my Life with the Liars

CAELA CARTER

HARPER

An Imprint of HarperCollins*Publishers*

To all the Curious little girls,
Especially Emma, Maria, and CC:
May you stay that way.

My Life with the Liars

For information address HarperCollins Children's Books, a division of HarperCollins Publishers, 195 Broadway, New York, NY 10007.
www.harpercollinschildrens.com

Library of Congress catalog card number: 2015938994
ISBN 978-0-06-238571-0 (trade bdg.)

Typography by Erin Fitzsimmons
16 17 18 19 20 PC/RRDH 10 9 8 7 6 5 4 3 2 1

First Edition

One

IT IS JUST LIKE FATHER PROPHET said it would be. The dark is everywhere, inky black above and below and to either side, squishing me back into the seat where the strap across my shoulder holds me, trapped. The man who is driving said I couldn't turn on the light. He said it would make it too hard for him to see the road. But I'm sure he was lying. The Outside is full of Liars and Darkness. That's what Father Prophet said.

"So, if you don't feel comfortable calling me 'Dad' yet, we can stick to my name for now," the man says. I don't want to look at him, but I do. Maybe the Darkness makes my head turn. There's gray fur on his jaw and his chin, which bounces up and down with his words. "My name is Louis." The fur is darker than the brown-gray of his hair.

Why would I call him Dad if his name is Louis?

I don't say anything. I won't. The Darkness can't make me. Curiosity is evil and conniving, but I won't let her find me. Not even here.

The car goes left. The lights in the front of us swing onto a new road. I turn and watch the white walls of the compound of the Children Inside the Light disappear from the window in the back. *Left turn,* I tell myself. *Big tree with dark green leaves across from the turn. Cactus with two shrugging shoulders on the other side.*

I have to know where I'm going. I have to be able to get back.

I pull my legs up to hug them, resting my chin on my knees. The road moves beneath the wheels hurling us down the street, farther and farther from safety. I'm not stupid and I remember all of the lists of vocabulary words we had to study for Outside Studies, so I know what this thing is.

> **Automobile** (n.): a passenger vehicle designed for operation on ordinary roads and typically having four wheels and a gasoline internal combustion engine

But I didn't know they felt this fast. I bite the edges of my lips until they bleed to keep my voice inside my mouth, to keep myself from screaming every time the machine careens around a turn or sails over a bump in the road.

"You doing OK, Zylynn?" the man asks.

I won't answer. I don't know how he knows my name.

He is an Agent of Darkness.

Back Inside, Father Prophet will be in the kids' building. They'll swarm around him, casting shadows all over his white clothes and pale skin, clamoring to get close, to be the one on his lap or sitting with their hands touching his huge calves through his white pants.

"We lost another," he will say. Will he cry?

Some of the kids will.

This is how it happened last week or month or something, when we lost Jaycia. "We lost another," Father Prophet had said. He didn't cry, but he almost looked like he would, like the Darkness had climbed into his soul and tried to sneak out of his eyes even though the ceilings and walls of the Girls' Dorm and the Boys' Dorm are always covered with bright, buzzing lightbulbs.

"We lost Jaycia," Father Prophet had said. He was holding my hand. I am always near him. "She lost her way."

For a minute, I thought of Jaycia. She was only a bit older than me, also twelve, also almost to her Rite of Passage. She was short with hair so light that if you held it off her head, you could see right through it. She would laugh when the Caretakers caught her doing something wrong. She was always doing something wrong. Not Abominations, not things that would get her cast out into the Darkness. Only Mistakes, like brushing her teeth for an extra thirty seconds or sneaking into the shower before I got a chance. I liked how she laughed. She slept in the bed next to me. I liked how she whispered at night, telling me about things I could barely imagine: bicycles, books, balloons. Things that only exist in the Darkness.

I think she was my friend, if I understand the word right.

Jaycia was lucky. She started in the Darkness, but she got rescued into the Light. I was luckier. I was born into the Light without the Darkness ever touching me.

Now neither of us is lucky.

"You know what she must do, right?" Father asked that day.

We nodded.

"She must keep her words to herself." He reminded us even though we knew. "She must leave as little of her voice out there in Darkness. She must focus all her efforts on returning here, where it is safe. If she tries hard enough to return, if she forces the Darkness out by thinking of us always, if she rejects all the temptations of Curiosity, if she keeps her soul in the Light, we'll see her again. If she tries hard enough before her thirteenth birthday, she'll return and she'll be able to live in the Light with us forever. But"—Father Prophet lowered his voice—"if we don't see her again, she has chosen Darkness and we must forget her."

Most of the other kids have forgotten her. She's stuck in Darkness forever now.

I won't be like Jaycia.

In the morning, there will be ten full days before my thirteenth birthday, before my ceremony. Ten days to get back and I know how to do it. I will think only of the Inside and Father Prophet and Mother God and Light, Light, Light. I will protect myself from the Liar. I will not listen to him or talk to him. I will keep my soul safe. If I have to, I'll yell at him, scream at him, hit him, hide, run away.

I will cast the Darkness so far away. I will be safe again in ten days, safe again in time.

It's only after minutes and hours that the car stops moving.

The man opens his door and gets out. "Come on, Zylynn," he says.

I sit and suck in the black air. With nothing but instinct, I try to feel behind me; I try to sense how far away Father Prophet and Inside and Light and everything I know are. I create a million invisible strings that wave around from my shoulders and back trying to find the white walls that kept the Darkness out, the dogs that barked at the gate, the other girls, Father Prophet, the Caretakers, Thesmerelda, the other women, anyone, anything that I left behind. The strings don't hit the Light. They sense nothing.

I strain to keep my heavy eyelids as far up into my head as they will go. I won't fall asleep in the Darkness, not when it's this black and scary.

The man walks away from the automobile. I watch him through the window as he crosses in front of it, his arms swinging in his red shirt with each step.

Whoever heard of a red shirt?

He keeps walking.

He's walking away. He's disappearing. He's going to leave me here. Then it will be just me and the Darkness for hours or days or more until Father comes to get me. I won't be able to eat or breathe or learn. I will die. My heart quickens, my blood rushes close to panic.

With a whoosh the door next to me opens. His face is right next to mine. I jump. I jump more than I need to so he won't see that I'm relieved he's still here. I shouldn't be relieved. "Come on, Zylynn. You're safe now. I promise."

His voice is so soft. It sounds like a nice voice.

But I know that it's not.

The first step into the house, he turns on a light. It scratches my eyes the way the lights do when I first wake up in the morning and the pain feels good. I follow him through a small, colorful room and into a kitchen. He turns on another light. I follow him through the kitchen to a hallway to a set of stairs. He turns on another light.

I am surprised.

I thought an Outsider would never let me see any light.

Inside, the kids will go to bed. The Caretakers will watch them and check off on the calendar when they drink their tea and wash their faces and brush their teeth and drink more tea and say goodnight. The kids, all in their matching large white T-shirts, will climb into their triple bunks and crawl under their white sheets and listen to the humming of the lights on the walls and the ceiling and watch the red on the inside of their eyes until they fall asleep.

Some of them might think about me in the Darkness.

Some of them might not.

Some of them will forget in a couple of days. Forget me.

It will all happen without me. Real life will happen without me.

There's only one bed in this room where I am now, in Darkness. The walls are white with pink stripes running up and down them. They're covered in what looks like wrapping paper, like the parcels Father Prophet gives us on our birthdays or on the Day of the Ultimate Feast.

The Agent of Darkness hands me a pile of pink cloth made of the softest furry fabric my fingers have ever felt. It lays in my palms and I don't know what I'm supposed to do with it. I look at the pink. Then, by accident, I look at him. His eyes are green and sharp.

"Get some rest," he says. "We'll work out everything in the morning."

In my head I say, *I'll run away in the morning if Father hasn't gotten me yet.*

"I'll do whatever I can to make you comfortable."

In my head I say, *I know you're lying. I will never believe you.*

The man crosses over the gold carpet and pauses at the doorway. He's looking at me. "Good night, Zylynn."

Then—just when I'm wondering how an evil Liar can have such a nice, soft voice—he turns out the light and closes the door so it's dark, dark, dark in the room.

I hold my breath and rush over to the switch on the wall. My heart is shaking in my chest. What if the light switch doesn't work? What if he's going to leave me in this blackness all night long? I flip it and the light comes back on. *Thank you, thank you.* I lean against the door, catching my breath.

I can't survive too long in the dark, that's what Father Prophet taught us.

So I can't run away now. The outdoor air is as black as the bruise on my left thigh. Father said the dark could hurt us, sting us, burn us, suffocate us. Father said nothing good happens in the dark.

I will run in the morning. If I'm still here. Maybe I won't be here. Father said if we wanted it enough, the Light would always find us. Until we turn thirteen.

I want you to come and rescue me, Father. I want it more than anything.

I look at the light trickling into the room. There's not enough. Just one measly lightbulb for a whole room. At home we had one hundred lightbulbs or six hundred lightbulbs or something in the dorms. But this little light is better than the black out the window. It's enough that the air turns smooth in my throat. Enough that my skin doesn't burn.

I stand in the center of the carpet where the light is brightest, right below the fixture on the ceiling. I look up at it until my eyes water, and I say the Evening Prayer.

Mother God,
Keeper of Light
Everything I have is yours; I choose to have nothing of my own.
I choose to be nothing but an Agent of your Light.

May the Darkness never find me.

I believe.

I say the prayer because it's evil to go to sleep without saying it. I say it because it's what I've said every day of my life. I say it because I want to please Mother God. But I stumble on the last line.

The Darkness has found me.

At home, where we sleep, there are lots of beds, thirty or one hundred. We can count, but we never did and now I can't remember exactly. There are bars of light on the ceiling and the walls. The beds are all white. The undersides of the beds are white. The room glows.

"Bright like a womb," says Father Prophet. "Bright like a child. Bright to keep you safe."

All the beds are filled with the Children Inside the Light every night . All the bright-white beds in the other dorm are filled with all the little boys. All the bright-white beds where I sleep are filled with all the little girls.

Except when they aren't.

Two

I AM SCREAMING WITH NO SOUND. I have been screaming with no sound for minutes or hours or days.

My eyes open.

There is light from the bulb on the ceiling, but it's not bright. Father Prophet has not come.

I don't know if it's time for waking because Brother Zascays, the Caretaker in the morning, will not come and wake us. I am not an "us." I am all alone. I have never been alone in a room before.

My feet touch the floor and it mashes beneath them. I know what this is because I go to school and I take Outside Studies and I can read and I have learned all about the World of Darkness so that I can be prepared if they ever come for me. I dig the word out of my brain from the lists of vocabulary we learned in school.

> **Carpet** (n.): a heavy fabric commonly of wool or nylon, for covering floors

I've never felt a carpet on my toes. It's not white. It's gold. It feels the same softness of the pink fabric and the Outsider's voice. I never thought the Outside would be soft, even a tricky, lying soft.

I am an evil, dirty girl for liking softness. I am an evil, dirty girl when I touch the pink fabric on the bed and when I wish my ears could hug and squish the Outsider's voice within them. Am I an evil, dirty girl if I walk on this carpet? There's no other way to walk.

There's no way not to hear the Liar's voice either.

I don't know if it is evil, but I do it anyway. I walk to the wall to look at the pink stripes. I try to hate the way the carpet sighs against the bottom of my feet. *I do try. I swear.*

The pink stripes please my eyes but I try to hate them too.

Maybe I'm not in Darkness. Maybe everything is OK. Maybe this whole room is Father Prophet's birthday gift for me, for my big thirteenth birthday, ten days early. I try to rip some of the paper away but it's stuck, not like the wrapping paper from my twelfth birthday, and I realize it's also probably a trick and a lie like Father Prophet said everything would be because this is Outside.

On the other wall, there's a window. I pull the curtain away and only see my face. It is still night. Still pitch-black outdoors without a hint of Mother God. I can't let that dark hit my skin. I can't run yet.

My face stares back from the black glass.

My green eyes stick so far out of their sockets it's like they're trying to escape. My cheekbones punch out of my pale skin and I think it might rip to let them through. My nose is huge now that my face has no fat. My yellow hair was just chopped yesterday or last month or something and it's clumpy, sticking to my scalp in one-square-inch pieces. I haven't seen myself in a long time, weeks or months or a year. I'm surprised at how old I look. How tired I look. How skinny I look.

But Father Prophet always liked my face. My Lightness, he called it.

I press my huge nose against the dark glass. The glass is black. Maybe this window is a lie too. Maybe it's not a window at all, but black glass glued against the pink-and-white wall. My breath shows up beneath my nose, a white fog painting lines against the blackness.

I like that I can create the white on the black. I do that until the glass turns a dark blue and trees and birds and the fastest automobile, the one from last night, start to appear. It is not a lie. It is a window. I know now.

At home we will start waking up soon. Or they will, without me. Because I'm not there. It's hard to remember.

The Caretakers will rouse the oldest girls first and we will crawl out of our tippy-top bunks, careful not to hit our heads on the ceiling. We'll grab towels from the hooks next to the pillows and take the bars of soap from the little ledges. We will leave all of the clothes we were wearing on the beds we sleep in and march, single file, out the swinging back door. The doors are made of screens and plywood. The floor is made of plywood too, and it's always covered in bits of sand.

The packed sand and dirt will be hot on the soles of our feet as we bounce across it to the bathroom behind the bunk. The first three of us will dash into the showers while the other girls line up behind. The Caretakers will go back into the bunks to rouse the medium girls, then finally the littlest girls who sleep closest to the floor.

We will each stand alone in a shower stall for three minutes until the buzzer goes off and the next girl comes in. The shower stall has no ceiling and no lightbulbs but the sun spills in and makes it bright enough. It's white: white walls, clear curtain.

The water will be sharp and cold. When it first hits our shoulders, it will feel like relief, but by the time it reaches our butts we'll be shivering. We'll each sandwich the white bar of soap between our palms to soften it, then we'll work it through our hair and around our faces and down each side of our bodies, gripping it tightly. When we hear a clunk of one bar of soap falling, we'll all feel a little sad. Because as soon as the soap falls, it gets sandy. And then that girl will have to live with sandy soap scratching her skin for a month until New Soap Day. And we'll be scared because we won't know what she did to make Mother God angry.

By the end of the month, we will all fail. All of the soaps will be sandy.

When the buzzer buzzes, we'll sprint into the toilet stalls to do our business. Some of the little girls will be crying in the back of the line, their bladders full to their throats. Some of them will have accidents. Little kids are the worst at obeying Father Prophet.

We'll line up, wrapped in towels, until everyone is through the shower and toilet. When we walk back across the hot sand, it'll almost feel good on our cold and wrinkly feet. We'll go back to the bunks and pull the clothes we left there onto our tacky skin, make sure the beds are neat, and line up again for breakfast.

We do all of that every day. Except today. Today we all do that without me.

I was maybe asleep against the window. I don't know. But the crackling of fat and the salty smell that sneaks under the door pulls me away from the now bright-light window. It's the sun making it bright, not the lights from Inside. It's like I'm in a shower instead of a room.

It's daytime again. Time to sneak out and go home.

But the crackling sounds and salty smell freeze my thoughts where they are.

I cross the carpet to stand with my face pressed against the door, trying to resist the smells and sounds. I shouldn't follow them. If I eat his food, I might have to talk to him.

I might hear his soft voice.

I might start to like him.

That is the ultimate evil, to like the Darkness.

It won't happen to me, Father Prophet. Hear me, please. Please, hear me.

But my stomach is stronger than my fear. It pulls me through the door and down that set of stairs.

I stand at the bottom and look down the short hallway into the bright kitchen. I like that it's bright. I like that it's full of noise: talking and chairs scraping and plates clinking.

But I can't trust that; I can't trust what I like.

There's a woman there. There are children too; I hear their voices. But I can see the woman through the door. She's about twenty feet away. Her back is to me. I can tell it's a woman by the way long hair is piled in curls on her head, by the curve of her backside in her jeans, by her high-pitched humming.

I haven't seen a woman in weeks or months.

She's by the stove. Flipping the bacon. It's her bacon. Woman's bacon. So can I eat it? Whenever Father Prophet warned us about the evil Outsiders who would try to get us and make us doomed and unsafe forever, he was talking about men. At least, I thought he was. But she is a woman. And there's bacon. It's like my birthday. Maybe it is my big thirteenth birthday, ten days early.

Maybe this is what's supposed to happen. Maybe this is the celebration that I've been preparing for, for almost thirteen years.

Except I know it's not, because there was no ceremony in the Chapel and none of the other girls ever got bacon. We only have bacon at the feasts.

The woman turns. Her face is like none I've ever seen before. Eyes that are as brown as the darkest part of the bacon. Skin the color of the pomegranate tea we drink before bedtime. A wide smile with the whitest teeth.

"Zylynn," she says. I don't know how they keep knowing my name. "Come in and join us. Would you like some breakfast?"

I nod. I want to get home. I need to leave. I will find a way to leave. But first, there's bacon.

I walk slowly into the brightness. It's almost as bright as our own Dining Hall, which has lights on the ceiling and the walls. But this kitchen only has lights on the ceiling.

When I cross the white tiled floor, the smell almost knocks me over. My stomach is singing as my nostrils suck it in greedily. There are three kids at the wooden table in the corner. They're smaller than me, much smaller, noisy and bouncy and they fall silent and stare at me when I walk in and I know that they will eat my bacon.

The woman turns with a plate in her hands. The plate is right at my elbow. There's bacon and other stuff. Strawberries. Something round and flat and tan.

"Here," she says like she thinks she's going to give me the whole plate and I know that has to be a trick or a lie or both. She's evil too. Father Prophet said not to trust anyone or anything in Darkness. He said not to give anyone any more words than you must to survive.

I need to get out of here. I need to run away.

But I also have to eat.

I take another step toward her, slowly. I raise my left hand, slowly. I raise my other one.

She stares at me like she doesn't know what I'm doing. Like she's never seen anyone eat before. Like she's waiting for the perfect moment to yell "Ha-ha!" and to make the food disappear.

But I'm smarter than she thinks. I'm smarter than she is.

Bam. The bacon—two whole strips—is in one hand, a strawberry is in the other. My feet are moving. Fast now. *Foot. Foot, foot, foot, foot.* Those kids won't catch me. That woman won't make my breakfast disappear. *Foot, foot, foot.* Out of the kitchen, down the hallway. *Boom, boom, boom,* go my feet up the stairs. Then I'm back in the room with the stripes.

I stand there with my back against the closed door and I stare at the treasures, the huge breakfast, the salty and sweet snacks. I am all alone, with food. I can eat slowly now. No one can come and steal them. No one can stop me.

Maybe it is good to sleep in a room with no one else.

My teeth sink into the bacon. It's salty. It's full of stuff, filly-up stuff. I can feel all the stuff as it falls from my tongue to my throat to my belly. Stuff that will line my stomach with relief.

On my second bite, he bangs a fist on the door and my head bounces against it. "Zylynn?"

I chomp again.

"Zylynn, sweetie? Come down. Have breakfast with us."

I lick the strawberry. Sweetness explodes against my taste buds. So much better than eating white, pasty oatmeal.

"You didn't get very much to eat, Zylynn."

I look at my hands. Two whole strips of bacon. One huge

strawberry. He's trying to trick me.

He'll come in here and take it back. He'll be in here any minute.

But he doesn't. Maybe he can't enter the Pink Stripes Room. Maybe Father Prophet stopped him somehow.

The man is gone. I eat one bite in peace before there's a tapping, like fingernails on the other side of the door. Long ones. Painted ones. "Zylynn?" It's the woman.

She might be tricking me too. She might be there saying my name so that he can come in and confuse me with lies until I am also a Liar and evil. "Zylynn?" Her voice is so high. "It's Charita. Can I come in?"

I step away. Then she's in the room.

When the women came home, there was a feast. Meat. Fruit. Sweets.

We would prepare for weeks, the men and the boys and the girls and the Gatherers-in-Training—the girls who are over thirteen but not yet old enough to go out into the Darkness every day. We would cook and decorate, like we were supposed to. There was a buzzing excitement that ran through our veins for days and days as we waited and waited for them to arrive. We were ready for the feast and the singing and the cheering and the games that always happened when the women came home.

They would descend on the Meeting Hall in the first circle, the one between the gates of the whitewashed wall and the

Girls' Dorm. The new souls that our women had brought with them would stare wide-eyed and scared because they weren't used to joy yet. They had never seen Light. We would sing and dance and throw flowers at them and celebrate.

The women who came back would hold us against their chests and rock back and forth, tears falling on our heads as they squeezed all of the Darkness out of their bodies.

The feast was always good. We would eat and eat and eat. And during the eating, each new grown-up member would present himself or herself to Father Prophet. They would kneel before him where he sat on his throne. They would lay everything they brought at his feet—money and jewels and electronics. All of the things that were making them greedy and keeping them in the Darkness. Then they would stand and Father would say, "Mother God welcomes you to her Light." And we would pause our eating to applaud. The new men would become Brothers and get a work assignment like Caretaker or Teacher or Messenger or Official to the Prophet. The new women train to be Gatherers.

The new kids would eat with us. Then they'd go back to the dorms with us. They'd be assigned their bed and their whites. They'd drink their tea. They'd go to sleep. Just like us. They'd be us.

After the feast was good too. It was always a long time until a Hungry Day or a pinging at the fence or any other sort of punishment. Mother God usually waited for the women to be home a few days before she punished us again.

But the women would be tired. They'd sleep in the Men's Dorms, all the way in the second circle, for days. They'd forget the singing. We'd go back to eating oatmeal and mushy pasta and potatoes and bread-and-lard for every breakfast and every dinner. We'd go back to regular days: mornings with the Caretakers, school with the Teachers, exercises with the Coaches, Coming to the Light with Father Prophet, bedtime prep with the Caretakers, sleep.

When the women were around, there were always hugs.

Father Prophet says that hugs are only for between a woman and a child. He says that's the only time Mother God is present. He says other hugs are "laying claim" and "laying claim" is the ultimate evil. So we'd go weeks and days and months with no hugs. Then there were hugs-hugs-hugs-hugs and just when our arms and bodies got used to it, the women would be gone again.

During the first days after the feast, the newest kids would tell us their names. Sometimes they got to keep them. Those names were short and sharp in our ears and on our tongues: Mark and Zach and Jill.

The boys and girls Father Prophet liked the most would get new names, ones that were soft and a whole bunch of beautiful sounds linked together. Like Thesmerelda. Like Jaycia. Like Zylynn.

During the first few days, when the women were still there, Father Prophet would come to the kids' building every night. He'd teach us a little lesson about the four most Ultimate Truths:

1. Everything good comes from Light.
2. Light, all Light, is Mother God and Mother God is all Light.
3. There is no Father except the Prophet; there is no Mother except God.
4. We belong to someone else.

"It's freeing," he'd say. "Soon you will see what true freedom is." He'd lead the bedtime prayer and tell us all good night. "Good night, Melhanisian." "Good night, Sharuma." "Good night, Zylynn."

Then he'd leave.

The babies would cry because they were addicted to Darkness.

We'd all fall asleep thinking of the hugs, hoping the women wouldn't be gone for so long the next time.

Now there is a woman in the striped-wrapping-paper room. She's holding that plate, the one I stole from, the one overflowing with food.

She takes a step toward me. I take a step back. Then another. Another.

I forget how the carpet feels soft against the soles of my feet until my back is pressed against the wall next to the window.

"I'm sorry you're afraid, Zylynn," she says. "Do you want your dad to come chat with us too?"

Dad is Louis, the Outsider, the soft voice, the one who drove me into the Darkness.

I shake my head.

Dad is scary. This woman is also scary. She's also an Outsider. She's also a Liar and evil and dirty.

She takes another step toward me. She's going to take my bacon. She's going to tell me to put the fat red strawberry back on that plate.

I take my palm and shove the fruit into my mouth, green stem and all. It's too big for my jaws. I stretch my lips over the parts of the berry protruding from between my teeth.

She looks at me with big eyes, like she's scared of me, like I'm the one from Darkness. I bite down on the fattest part of the strawberry and juice runs down my throat and between my lips and down my chin. The little seeds crunch between my teeth. My entire mouth—taste buds, teeth, tongue, throat, lips—is singing for joy, but the rest of my body is trembling so much I can hear my bones clink against each other.

The woman takes another step closer. I can't back up anymore. If she tries to touch me, I will jump out the window.

She puts the plate down on the little table next to the pink bed.

"I'm not going to hurt you, Zylynn. Neither is your dad," she says. "We won't do anything you don't like, OK?"

Her voice is so nice and slippery and musical and I want to believe her. But I can't. Because they already did something I don't like. They already took me away, into the Darkness.

She keeps talking. "If you want to eat in your room, that's OK," she says. My room. I wonder if she thinks the pink stripes are mine. I wonder how she doesn't know that nothing can belong to me because I belong to someone else. "Why don't you finish your breakfast and then we'll get you cleaned up and into some clean clothes?"

I look down at what I'm wearing, our clothes. The ones we always wear. White T-shirt, white undershirt, white underwear, white shorts. I look back up at her. These clothes were just cleaned some number of days ago. There are only a few dirty gray streaks on my shorts; my T-shirt is not even that yellow yet.

"Do you want more breakfast?" she asks.

She looks at the plate on the table. So do I. I still have the piece of bacon in my fist. I still have a little strawberry on my tongue; the green part is wedged between my molars. But the plate is exploding with colors and smells and more food than I've ever seen in one spot. She seems to think it's all for me. She seems stupid.

Or that's all the food I'll ever get. Maybe that's my food until I figure out how to escape. Maybe that's my food for up to ten days.

I nod.

"Do you want to eat it alone?"

I nod again.

She's gone. The plate is still here.

Three

FATHER PROPHET STILL HAS NOT COME.

It's a few hours later, I think. The Liars are everywhere I look, in every room, in every place. I can't get out of here.

I don't know what else to do. I don't want to open my mouth and leave my voice here, my mark here, myself here in the Darkness. So I follow their directions, I do what they say, while in my brain I promise Father Prophet over and over that I'm not forgetting him.

Charita runs me a bath. I've never seen a bath before, but I know what one is. Then she leaves me all alone in the bathroom, but she takes my clothes, so there's no way I can run away now. The bathroom is not-quite-white everywhere and the lights on the ceiling are bright, almost like the lights at home. They reflect and bounce off the floor and the walls and the tub, which is also white and right in the same room as the toilet and sink.

I sit in the tub. All alone in the room. It's so weird to be alone.

The hot water swishes around my body, pulling dirt off my skin and turning me soft and wrinkly. I rub the orange washcloth against my face, my bony cheeks and jaw and chin, and I scrub until everything feels raw and sore and new.

I like the bath.

I like the three strips of bacon, the two strawberries, the one round-and-flat circle thing with the sticky brown sweet stuff that are now sitting in my stomach making it feel warm and full and comfy.

I like the other two strips of bacon, the other two circle things, and the other four strawberries that are hidden on the plate under the bed in the Pink Stripe Room.

I know that all of these things are lies. They're tricks. I know that as soon as I start to believe them the Darkness will descend and the Outsiders will finally reveal themselves to be the evil people they are. I know.

I can't help what pleases my eye or what feels good on my skin.

But I won't like them so much that I believe in them. I won't like them so much I start to trust that they will stay.

I won't.

"We live in the evil state of America," Father Prophet said in Chapel soon after Jaycia was taken. "We live in a state where choice belongs only to those who are at least eighteen years of age, where if they get you they will not understand the urgency of your thirteenth year. Every one of you has found the Light, regardless of your youth. The Light is the most important thing about you. Outside our compound is a Dark state that does not understand that Light will ultimately win."

We, all the kids, sat on the benches in the front of the Chapel like always. In the early morning, the stone was hard and cold against the bones in our butts and backs. Father Prophet was talking about Jaycia. Even though a lot of the kids had forgotten her already.

I tried to remember her. I tried imagining her blond hair and her blue eyes and her laugh, which always felt like soap bubbles floating from the bed next to mine.

I worried that if it wasn't for the Abomination, I'd be one of the kids who forgot her completely.

"The Light will always win in the universe," he said. "But the Darkness can win in you. It wins in thousands of souls who choose to stay far away. It wins in anyone who spends his or her childhood here, but is not here, with me, on this stage when she turns thirteen, when he turns thirteen."

We felt a shiver go up our spines. Not being here at sunset when we turn thirteen: we couldn't imagine anything worse.

After we turn thirteen, we start training to do the Work. The teen boys train for different things: as Cooks or Caretakers or Coaches or Officials who help Father Prophet all day long. The teen girls train to Gather Souls. They all go to school with us, but only in the morning. In the afternoons, we can see the thirteen-, fourteen-, fifteen-, sixteen-, seventeen-, eighteen-, nineteen-year-old boys all over the compound, helping out all of the Brothers. Preparing to be Brothers themselves in one way or another. The teen girls spend afternoons in another classroom where they learn how to go Outside. How to guard themselves against the dark. What to say in order to earn new souls, to make people follow them into Mother's Light.

Once we turn thirteen—even though we still go to school and train—we're not kids anymore. We're real. We're a part of the Light.

We wait our whole lives to stand on that stage in our Ceremony. And if we aren't there at that moment, if we don't turn those Lights on with Mother God, our whole life was a waste.

"You all choose to be here, right?" Father Prophet said. "You each choose to be here, right? In the Light?"

We nodded. We all nodded. We always nodded.

Charita knocks on the bathroom door. *Clomp, clomp, clomp.* She's not using her nails this time but I can still tell it's her because I can see her because the door is mostly open. I don't have to say anything or get out of the tub. She stands in the doorway.

"Zylynn? How you doing in here? Almost clean?"

I bite my scabby lip. I was hoping Father Prophet would come for me before I had to get out of the tub. I've been praying and praying and praying to him.

"Here," she says. She's leaning against the door with slips of color folded into her arms. "I brought you some clothes for when you're all clean."

She shows me denim shorts and a pink shirt with buttons

up the middle. She pulls a pair of purple underwear out of a plastic package. "These are all new, see?" she says, holding up the package.

I keep my words locked up.

I can't like the clothes. I won't.

I pull the bar of soap—smooth, not sandy, from the bottom of the tub where I was hoping it would soften, I put it to my head to show her I still have to wash my hair. She lowers her eyebrows.

"What are you doing?" Charita says.

I rub the soap against my skull until I can feel the first bubbles tickling my fingers.

Charita rushes through the door. "Oh, sweetie. Oh, Zylynn, stop. We have shampoo."

I open my palm. The soap plunks back into the water.

"I'm sorry, if you want me to go I'm—anything you need you can let me know, OK? Including privacy."

Privacy . . . privacy . . . privacy . . .

I've never learned that word.

I won't wonder about it. I'm not curious. Curiosity is nearby but I won't let her catch me.

"You're almost thirteen, I know. I have to keep reminding myself that you're older than my kiddos downstairs."

They know. The Liars know how old I am. They know how close it is to my time.

"So, anyway, I'm sorry. I'll get out of your hair, but—" She plucks a plastic bottle with pink goop filling about half of it off the edge of the tub and hands it to me. "Here. Shampoo."

My hand is slippery and the bottle splashes into the water but I fish it back out. I stare at the label.

> **Shampoo** (n.): a liquid or cream prepared for the washing of hair or carpets

I know what it is. We know what everything is (except privacy and I'm sure we were about to learn that one). Only I don't know how to use it.

"OK?" Charita freezes by the tub. She won't leave until I say something.

I snap the bottle open and smell it. Strawberry jam. She wants me to put it in my hair?

"If you don't like it we can get you something else."

Why is she speaking so fast? Why is she jittery like I make her nervous? If she doesn't like me, will she let me go home?

"Do you like it?" she asks.

I look at her.

"Sweetie . . . do you want . . . should I help?"

I can't answer. I don't want to talk. She won't leave if I don't answer. I don't know what to do. *Get here, Father. Get here now. Help me.*

She leans over the tub and her fingers rest on the top of the bottle. I loosen my grip. I let her slip it out of my palm.

Then it's my head under the pitcher as she pours water through my hair. It spills down my neck and back in warm rivers. Her fingers work suds through the clumps on my head until they separate and she spends extra time rubbing my scalp until I feel as smooth as a bar of soap on New Soap Day. When it's over, my head feels lighter.

But my heart feels heavier. Guilty. Guiltier.

Back in the kitchen.

The colorful fabrics slip against my skin. The cushion of the kitchen chair whispers nice things to the bones in my butt. The new socks and sneakers hug my feet. Lies.

There are three other kids sitting at the table. They stare at me. Charita and Louis are busy behind my head, opening and shutting the refrigerator, turning on and off the sink faucet like they have all the water in the world. They won't stop talking, their words filling up all of the space in my head where I'm trying to keep up my pleas to Father.

"Junior?" Charita says. "Peanut butter and jelly? With carrot sticks."

"Yes, please," the oldest one says. He has curly hair that flops over his ears and forehead. It's so dark. He has green eyes. His hair bounces on his head when he talks.

"Elsie?" Charita says.

"Can I have turkey? With mustard? And tomato?" the girl says. Her brown hair is divided into two braids that hang next to her ears. My own hair sticks up from my scalp in every angle, all of the hairs separate now that Charita washed out the clumps. My hair has never been long enough for braids because I have never been thirteen and I haven't had my ceremony and I'm not a woman yet so it's right and perfect for my hair to keep getting chopped. Elsie's shirt looks like mine, only it's green. She has green eyes. Also like mine. And Junior's.

"Jakey?"

"Peanut butter!" the little one screams from his high chair.

I jump at his loudness and they stare at me again. I've never heard words be so loud. Usually noises that are that loud are crying or angry or nightmares.

The little one hides his own green eyes behind his tiny fingers.

My stomach gurgles even though it's still full of breakfast. I won't be getting any food. There can't be that much food out in Darkness. It can't be the way they're making it seem, like their fridge has no back wall, like it goes on and on, like it's a cold cave filled with all sorts of meats and fruits and vegetables. The Agents of Darkness will make me sit here and watch these squeaky-clean kids with the dark hair eat and eat and eat while they laugh at me behind my head. They want my stomach to churn and ache so that it feels like it's eating itself.

But they aren't that smart out here in the Darkness. My stomach is still full from before.

"Zylynn?" Charita says. "Is peanut butter and jelly good for you too?"

I nod, wide-eyed. I can't believe it. I don't know what jelly is, but it is good. Food is good.

Food shouldn't be good in Darkness. I don't know how to make it not-good. I know it's a lie, but I still don't know how to hate it. *I'm sorry, Father. Help me.*

I need to go home. Time is running out. But I can't run away now; they would notice and snatch me right back up. I have to wait until they leave me alone while the sun is up and while I have clothes on. *Help me, help me!*

Charita puts a white plate in front of each of us kids. Each plate is different. Mine is the only one with strawberries on it.

"I noticed you liked them at breakfast," she whispers over my ear.

I turn and stare at her.

Each of the other kids says thank you. My mouth stays shut. They start eating. So do I. I shove a huge mouthful of bread mushed with peanut butter and something purple into my mouth before they can take it away. Louis comes next to me and sits. I know he's going to take the plate away. He's going to laugh at me for liking the food and the bath and the clothes and the way there's a woman right in the same room with us. I try to shove more food in.

"Take it easy there, Zylynn," he says. His green eyes are rimmed with red. His eyebrows look more gray than they did yesterday. His fur is mostly gone. "This isn't a race."

I stare at him.

"Does she know how to talk?" Junior says.

Is the "she" me? How could he think that? I'm bigger than he is once or twice over. Of course I know how to talk. I know how to speak and read and count and find the Light and a million other things that there's no way little Junior knows.

"I'm not stupid," I say. The words slip from my mouth and line themselves up on the table. They stare at me. They are the proof that I am really here, far away from everything that is real and Light and safe.

Those are the first words I say in the Darkness. And they come out all jumbled because I have to push them through a mouth sticky with peanut butter.

I take a sip of rich, creamy milk. A lie. *I know it's another lie, Father.*

"I'm not stupid," I say again. "I know more than you do."

The kids stare at me. We all chew.

The girl says, "Is our father really your father?"

I almost smile. They're the ones who think I'm stupid. But I stay serious. It's not Elsie's fault she was raised in Darkness. That was a big lesson from Outside Studies. We have to try to win souls, young souls. The doomed children in the Darkness can become lucky Children Inside the Light. They're not the evil Liars; they're the victims.

I tell her the Ultimate Truth. The thing that you must know and believe in order to be in the Light. The piece of knowledge without which it is not worth living. I say, "There is no Father except the Prophet; there is no Mother except God."

Her eyebrows jump. She looks confused. She maybe looks scared.

Maybe, when Father Prophet comes to find me, I can take

her back with me. I can become a Gatherer early. Maybe I can start doing the Work before I even turn thirteen. Father Prophet would be so proud. He'd forgive me for being in the Darkness and eating the food and taking a bath with shampoo.

I say it again. "Did you hear me? There is no Mother except God, no Father except the Prophet."

Louis sighs.

Elsie takes another bite.

I'll save her.

I'll get myself home. And I'll take her with me.

The worst days Inside were the Hungry Days.

They started like all the other days. We would wake up at the Caretaker's whistle and we'd crawl out of our beds and shift our way through hot sand, freezing showers, and hard toilets. We'd march the five minutes to the next building in the first circle. We'd sit at the long kids' table in the Dining Hall with the electric lights buzzing over our heads and to our right and left and front and back, and nothing would show up.

The Cooks would come out of the kitchen in the back. Their hands would be empty. Their mouths would be straight. "Be brave," they'd say. "Ask for forgiveness."

On Hungry Days the sticky, pasty oatmeal in our brains was the most delicious meal we'd ever thought of.

On Hungry Days we would go to school and write answers on our chalkboards and read our pamphlets or listen to lessons and learn and try not to think about our stomachs folding themselves in half over and over again. We'd try not to listen to all of the folding stomachs around us as they grumbled through the classroom.

On Hungry Days, during Exercise, we would end up lying on the mats, clenching our middles while a fire ripped through them one after the other. We'd try not to cry out loud. We'd usually fail.

On Hungry Days we didn't even go into the Chapel for prayer. On Hungry Days Father Prophet was never around.

Hungry Days were his way of reminding us of our Inadequacies and Abominations. They were his warning about what would happen if we forget him.

I thought I'd already been punished. I'd hoped the string of Hungry Days after all the strangers left was enough to punish me.

But my Abomination was really bad.

And now I'm in Darkness.

Four

WHEN JUNIOR TAKES ELSIE AND JAKEY down the stairs in the back of the kitchen and Charita and Louis turn their backs to put some plates in the sink, I take my sandwich and run out the front of the kitchen, up the stairs, and into the Pink Stripes Room.

I bend over the bed and pull out the breakfast plate. I scoop the round-and-flat circle thing and five more strawberries into my hands and clutch the food to my chest.

Go down the road, I remind myself. *Make a left at the end of it. Walk until you see the shrugging cactus.*

Wait.

Was the shrugging cactus on the next road? The third or the second road?

And is it a left if I'm coming from this way? Or was it a left when we drove here?

"Whatcha doing there, Zylynn?" Louis's voice says behind my head.

I'm still hunched next to the bed holding all of the food. The air rushes out of me. I drop the food onto the plate.

I missed my chance.

How will I escape when I don't know where to go? *Please come get me, Father.*

I stand still, make my back rigid, like it's pressed against one of the wooden boards of the Inside classroom that we have to stand between if we forget an answer. I make my eyes huge and innocent. I trick him.

"How was your lunch?" He says it like it's normal. He says it like Lunch is something that happens every day.

"Good," I say to distract him. He's so delighted by my word that he misses it as the toe of my new sneaker shoves the rest of the white plate under the bed.

He takes a step toward me, then another one, then another like he's going to be right next to me and sit on the bed or something, and he can't sit on the bed because I might need to sleep in it tonight and I don't want to sleep in it if a Liar has touched it.

I look at him and he freezes.

"Do you understand what's happening, Zylynn? Do you want to ask me anything?"

That's not fair. Those are two questions with two different answers. He's trying to make me speak as many words as possible. He's trying to use my voice to fill up his Darkness.

It's hard to remember that I'm in Darkness with the way the sunshine is streaming through the open window behind me. But Father Prophet said that the Darkness is always tricky. I have to be trickier.

"I don't have any questions," I say.

"Do you understand what's happening?" he asks again.

This time I nod. I'm lying, but he's the Liar. It's so confusing.

Louis sighs.

"The kids went to play outside," he says.

I don't understand because we are Outside. Everything is Outside. And it's the middle of the day. Don't we have to go to school and exercise?

"Do you want to join them? There's a swing set out there. You might be a little old for swing sets. I guess I haven't figured out everything . . . what we'll do now . . . everything you'll need . . . a twelve-year-old girl will . . . whatever you need you'll have . . . I'll—we'll—try . . ."

I can't let the words in my ears, the soft slipperiness of them, the way they're wiggling into my brain and getting comfortable, the way they're promising the things we've never been promised, the way they know things about me like how old I am and my name, the way they coat my skull like they are meant for only me, like I am something all by myself.

I walk past him and down the stairs and he follows me but he stops talking so it's OK or it's at least better. I walk through the hallway and through the kitchen past Charita and out into the sunlight where the three kids are exercising.

Come and get me, I beg Father Prophet. *Come and get me soon. I'm sorry for what I did.*

* * *

Their compound is small. I think about tha
ing on the fence in the back of it with the th
back and forth in front of my face in some sort of cha
undirected form of Exercise.

If I were at home, Inside, I would be in charge of these three because I am the biggest and therefore probably the oldest. I don't know if I'm supposed to be in charge of Junior and Elsie and Jakey. I don't know if I'm supposed to be changing their spazzy game into productive Exercise that will increase their heart rates and build their muscles and help their blood flow and remind them to ask Father Prophet to thank Mother God for their bodies.

But I don't care if I'm in charge here because I'm in Darkness and I'm supposed to hate everything.

I hate everything, Father.

This compound is just one building. The people here eat and bathe and sleep and dress and work and do business and pray and smile and worship and sing and talk and laugh and learn and cook and clean and breathe all under only one roof. If they do all those things. And all the other things they maybe do also. Only one roof. I know because I can see that the fence I'm standing against goes around only this one building. They call it *house.*

House (n.): a building in which people live; a residence for human beings

There are only five people on the whole compound: Louis and Charita and Junior and Elsie and Jakey. I'm trying to hate them. But it's hard to hate the kids who laugh like Jaycia while they're running back and forth under a stream of water that juts out of a silver thing in the middle of the yard. They call it *sprinkler.*

I look around, out over the fence to the street. That's where I will go to escape. I flip the palm of my left hand so it's facing up and try to draw a map on it with my right pointer finger. There's only one way to go on this road because this compound rests on the curved end of it. So I know the first step. At the end of the road, I'm pretty sure I turn left.

Were there three roads total? Or four?

I remember turning at a shrugging cactus.

Help me, Father. Help me.

Suddenly the three kids are all in a pile in the middle of the yard, about four feet in front of me. They're loud. It's a squeaking, screeching kind of loudness that isn't words like it was when Jakey asked for peanut butter and it isn't crying and they aren't asleep so it isn't a nightmare. It's a painful, piercing, useless sound and then I hear Elsie say "Stop! Stop!"

This is something I've seen before. It's something I know the word for. I flip through the lists of vocabulary words that I've learned in school. I can't find the right one.

Elsie gets louder: "Stop! Stop!"

Maybe I am in charge.

She screams again.

I may be supposed to hate Elsie but I don't. She's too small and sweet with a smile and freckles and eyes like mine. And if I can teach her and take her back with me and make her part of the rest of us, then I won't be allowed to hate her anymore. If I use her to get Father to forgive me, then I'll have to forgive her.

I don't want her to get hurt.

I run over and stand a foot away. The two boys are on their feet with their fingers on her legs and arms and she's wiggling and squiggling and so, so loud and the "Stop! Stop!" sounds like a nightmare sounds. But Elsie is also smiling with so many teeth like Jaycia did. Whenever I hear the "Stop! Stop!" in the middle of the night I'm supposed to wake the girl up and let her remember that she is safe Inside, she is in the Light. Elsie isn't in the Light but maybe I could take her into the Light but not if she's loud and screaming like that and not if she's hurt and it sort of doesn't look like they're hurting her but it sounds like they are and I can't remember what this is called, the word, but I know that it's bad and no matter what it's called and no matter if I hate them I don't want anyone to hurt anyone. So I do it.

I leap toward the kid-pile, sailing through the air headfirst with my arm out to the side. I land next to Junior, my arm anchoring his hand to his hip. The force of my shoulder slams into his throat and knocks him into the grass. I use my hands to pin his elbows down to the ground and then Elsie is free.

And I remember the word.

Fight (v.): to contend in battle or physical combat. Esp: to strive to overcome a person by blows or weapons

There were fights Inside when new kids arrived. Only then. Those kids were still addicted to Darkness. They sometimes got confused and then they got angry and then they screamed and kicked and punched, until they remembered Father Prophet and they'd stop.

This was a fight. Of course it was. These kids are all addicted to Darkness.

The next second, while I'm holding Junior to the ground and he's beneath my palms, is the quietest one in Darkness so far. All three of them stare at me, six green eyes wide and weird and six brown eyebrows arched high into three cinnamon-colored foreheads.

Then Junior is crying. It's loud but at least I know what it is.

I don't know what to do. I don't know how they punish fighting here. I don't even know if fighting is against the rules. I don't know anything.

My skin feels like it's burning where it's touching Junior, so I let him up.

Elsie and Jakey are crying now where they sit in the grass. All three of them sit and cry. Elsie cries the loudest. I look at her, confused. She should have been crying before. Now I rescued her. Now it's time to stop being loud.

Then Louis and Charita are there with us saying, "What happened? What happened?" and I wonder if words are this loud on every Outside compound or only on this one.

Charita is looking at me. She's holding on to Elsie, squeezing her. "What happened?" she says to me again, not soft anymore.

I don't want to use my voice. I don't want to leave my words here. I don't want to be here.

Please, take me away. You can do anything. I believe in you. I'm sorry and I want to be with you.

I watch Charita holding Elsie. I watch her spreading her arms like they can go on forever and then I watch her holding all three of the kids on her one-and-only lap. It looks like when the women come home after a long, long time. But it also looks different. Somehow. She's holding them the same way. She's kissing their heads the same way. But they're the ones crying.

When the women hugged us, the grown-ups cried and little kids squirmed in their arms. When the women hugged us it was like they were latching on to our Light after a long time in Darkness.

But this hug looks different. The kids are latching on to Charita. It's as if the hug is for them and not for her.

What does it feel like to be held like that?

When she asks again, her voice is quieter. "What happened, Zylynn?"

I answer. "They were fighting." Forty-seven, forty-eight, forty-nine words out here in Darkness.

I'm sorry, Father.

Charita looks down at the kids, three little heads gathered under her nose. "Tickle fighting," Junior says quietly. "We were tickle fighting."

Tickle. I scan through lists and lists of vocabulary words. *Tickle.* I don't know that one.

There was a sound coming from the next bunk over. We didn't know what it was.

I rolled over. "Are you crying?" I asked.

"No," Jaycia said. "Laughing."

I located the word in my head right away.

Laugh (v.): to emit a sound of joy, merriment, or amusement

We hadn't heard a real laugh before.

"Why?" I whispered. I was in charge in the bright sleeping room. I was the oldest besides Jaycia, and she was the newest so she couldn't be in charge. Father Prophet said Zylynn was in charge. Zylynn was supposed to stop any whispering; Zylynn was supposed to end any nightmares; Zylynn was supposed to keep it bright-light and quiet until the Caretakers came back in the morning.

But no one told me what to do about laughter.

"I was remembering this one joke my dad told me once," she said. "Want to hear it?"

I knew it was a Mistake to talk during the nighttime. Too many Mistakes would make Father angry. I knew I should say no and tell Jaycia to go to sleep. But would her joke make me laugh too? What would it feel like to have that bubbly sound pass through my own windpipe?

"Why didn't the skeleton cross the road?" Jaycia said.

"Is that the joke?" I asked.

"No, now you ask why," she said.

"Why?" I asked.

"Because he didn't have the guts."

Jaycia laughed again. Was this the part where I joined in? Was this the part where the bubbly noise was supposed to come from my own belly? Was it like crying, which happened whether you wanted it to or not, or like talking, which only happened when you told your body to do it?

I tried it. I made a sound in my stomach that jabbed my throat on the way out. It didn't sound bright and lovely.

It made Jaycia wrinkle her nose at me.

Maybe we didn't have laughter.

It's nighttime again.

First, the sun set. I saw it sinking down the sky. And I was trapped again. If I ran away, I'd get stuck in the dark and I'd suffocate or burn or something.

There was more food, then there was more going "outside" but I wouldn't do it. I sat under the electric bulb in the living room and prayed and begged and pleaded and planned. But I didn't come up with anything. I don't know how to get out of here.

Then there were some strange bedtime prayers. Then there was brushing teeth and other normal things. Then there was bed.

A whole day in Darkness and I still don't know the rules. Inside, we tell the new people all of the rules right away.

I stand under the weak lightbulb in the Pink Stripes room.

Mother God,

Keeper of Light

Everything I have is yours; I choose to have nothing of my own.

I choose to be nothing but an Agent of your Light.

May the Darkness never find me.

I believe.

I put on the pink clothes tonight. They feel like clouds against my skin.

I get under the thick blanket. Its weight is like one of the women hugging me. Like Thesmerelda hugging me.

I think about the pancake (I finally figured out the word), the five strawberries, the three strips of bacon, the half peanut butter and jelly sandwich, the four chicken fingers from dinner under the bed. I think about the stuff I couldn't steal—mac and cheese and milk—in my belly.

I hate it here, Father. I really hate it.

It's confusing and upside down and pointless. Everything good is a trick. Everything bad is real.

I close my eyes and scary things fly through my brain: the fastest car ever, the dogs at the gate, the shampoo falling into the water . . . Jaycia climbing out of her bed for the last time . . . the moon on the night of the Abomination . . .

I tremble in the new clothes and new bed until I'm sure I'll never sleep.

Five

I'M FINALLY ASLEEP AND THEN I'M not anymore. The window is still black, the lightbulb's reflection shining off it.

Again, I'm awake in the middle of the night and alone so I could run away without being caught, but I'm trapped by the Darkness on the other side of the window.

Noises sneak into the room. My head is only a foot from the wall because the bed I'm sleeping in is flush against it. The noises get louder, then quieter, then louder, then quieter. It's voices. Charita and Louis.

At home, the walls are covered in lights and the lights buzz and the buzzing sounds like something safe and warm and close and it helps me sleep. Here in the silence the voices outside the wall can come wandering in through the pink stripes whether you were sleeping or whatever you were doing.

And there's no tea.

"I know," Louis's voice is saying. "I know. I did it all wrong."

"Louis, she's lost. She's almost thirteen and she knows

nothing about the world." Charita's voice is louder. I've never heard a woman sound so loud. Or angry.

"What do you want me to do? She's my daughter."

Daughter. I flip through the in-brain vocabulary lists for that one. I can't find it. But I think the "she" is me. Me, Zylynn. Me, all by myself. Me, alone in Darkness. I am *daughter.*

"Louis!" Charita yells this, yells his name like he doesn't know who he is or like he needs to come over to her even though they're in the same room and he's already talking to her.

I know what this is. It isn't a fight because there are no blows or weapons. Just words.

"We aren't talking about what to do now," she says. "How did it get this bad? Why was she there for so long?"

Quarrel (n.): a verbal altercation between two antagonists

There's quiet now, muffling.

I hate that I don't understand what they're talking about. It makes me feel stupid.

"It got so much worse," Louis says finally. The words barely find their way between the pink stripes and into my head. I sit up in bed to try to catch them in my ears, but I don't know why. I didn't want to hear them when they started. I don't know what they mean.

His voice is soft like always.

"Back when I lived there, back when I was a part of the

Movement . . . or whatever . . . I mean, we lived in the same place. We had our own room, two parents and a kid . . . it was on the compound but it was still . . . more . . . normal . . . Inside . . ."

Louis used to live Inside?

"I'm not defending myself," he says. "I . . . It was the worst thing I ever did . . . going there . . ."

"I know, babe, I know," Charita says.

"And . . . leaving her there . . . leaving my daughter . . ."

Daughter. Me again? *Daughter.* He didn't leave me there. He took me away.

Louis is still talking. I can hear most of it now. "But it wasn't as bad as . . . when I went back there, I didn't . . . I wasn't . . . prepared. It was so much worse . . ."

"Oh, baby," Charita says and I don't know why because there's not a baby on this entire compound unless Charita and Louis have been hiding it from me in whatever room they're in now that's next to the pink stripes.

"I thought I'd leave her as long as I could . . . I hated the thought of taking her from her mother . . ."

There is no Father except the Prophet; there is no Mother except God.

"She doesn't even know who her mother is," Charita says.

My Mother is God.

Her voice is softer now. I wonder if the quarrel is over. "She doesn't know anything. She's terrified. What are we going to do with her?"

"Do you want me to take her back?"

I hear Louis ask it and I sink into the bed. I pull the blanket over my head and I breathe hot air out into the little soft cave I just made for myself.

He'll take me back. Just like that. After only one full day in Darkness, tomorrow he'll take me back.

I allow myself a smile. I did it.

Thank you, Father. I knew I wouldn't forget you. I knew it.

"I don't want to be here," Jaycia said at breakfast during her first week. "I don't want to be like you."

We all squinted at her.

"My mom is making me," she said.

We didn't know that word. Mom.

We tilted our heads. We squinted more.

"What?" she said. "I don't want to be like you with your icky oatmeal and your bright, bright bedroom and your weird ideas about God. I want to be Janice again. I want it to be like I used to be."

"But," I said.

"But," we all said.

"But what?" Jaycia asked.

"But we're right," I said.

"There's not a right like that," Jaycia said. "Not everything is just right and wrong. Sometimes things can be about what you want."

"We want to be here," I said.

"I'm not talking about you!" Jaycia said, a little too loudly. We weren't breaking any rules. We were allowed to talk at breakfast. We weren't saying anything that would invite Curiosity. We weren't being greedy or violent.

But it felt like we were breaking a rule.

"I'm talking about me, about what I want," Jaycia went on. "You can want to be here, fine, fine, fine. Just because Thesmerelda brought you here so long ago and you know how to like it or something. But I can't do it. I can't like it. I hate it."

"Thesmerelda?" I asked. What did she have to do with anything?

"She's your—"

"STOP," I shouted at Jaycia. We weren't supposed to say "my" or "your." It was the most bad thing ever to say "my" or "your" about another person. The worst Abomination. Thesmerelda can't be my anything because she belongs to Mother God.

Jaycia kept talking. "I want to be home. I miss my dog. I'm missing so much school. I don't know what movies have come out, what my friends are wearing for Halloween. I miss everything. I want to go home."

I was the oldest at the table. I had to handle this. And I didn't want to turn her over to the Gatherers-in-Training, the teen girls. They were usually the ones who dealt with it when the new people had too many questions. I didn't know exactly how, but the new souls always stopped asking questions after they dealt with the Gatherers-in-Training.

"But—" I said.

"I know, Zylynn, I know, OK?" Jaycia said. "I know you're going to lecture me about the dangers of wondering, how that's too close to Curiosity and how she's some evil who tempts you away from the Light. But you can save your breath, OK? Because I don't believe any of this."

"But—"I said.

"But what, Zylynn? But what?"

"But we're right," I said.

We all nodded.

We went back to eating oatmeal.

Jaycia sighed.

Later, she learned. Eventually we all learned.

Now I'm awake. It's morning. The sunlight is falling in through the window and there are no words sneaking through the walls. It's quiet but it's morning. That's the opposite of how it's supposed to be. Mornings are supposed to be full of noise. Not loud, but noisy with the "good mornings" and the water for the washing and the sound of feet against the sand. Nights are supposed to be quiet except for the lights buzzing. Everything in Darkness is backward.

Somehow I fell asleep again last night, but first, for hours, I hid under that blanket with a racing heart, praying to Father and promising that I remember everything. I fell asleep, then woke up, then fell asleep, then woke up. So many times.

When I wake up to the sun and the quiet, I'm happy. And it's not because my bed is all warm and snuggly. It's not because my pillow smells like strawberry shampoo.

It's because I remember what Louis said last night. And today I'll get back into her Light.

I did so well, I'll make it back to Father with eight days to spare.

Minutes and hours pass before Louis knocks on the door. I'm sitting on the edge of the bed studying the pink stripes to try to keep them in my memory for as long as I can once I'm back. Father Prophet wouldn't like that, but the pink stripes aren't evil or dirty or Liars, they're just stripes. And I want to remember them.

I'm dressed in the outfit they gave me yesterday, shoes and all, my hair combed back on my head. Hours ago while the house was still sleeping but the sun was awake in the windows, I tiptoed to the bathroom so that I won't have to go before we leave. I'm ready. Father Prophet won't like my clothes, but he'll be so proud of me for getting back so quickly that he'll give me a new white T-shirt and shorts.

"Zylynn?" Louis whispers. "Are you awake?"

I won't answer.

The door opens anyway. "Look at you!" he says, his voice doing a weird up-and-down thing that makes my stomach turn. But it doesn't matter. He's taking me home now. "Up bright and early like the sun!"

He smiles at me so hard, I shrug.

I stand to go.

"I'm off to work," he says. "Just wanted to say good-bye before I head out."

My heart falls so fast I'm sure he can hear it clunk when it hits the floor. He's a Liar. How could I have ever believed that he was telling the truth? Even if he was talking to Charita.

He stares at me, his green eyes squinting, his lips curved into question marks.

"Is that OK, sweetie . . . Zylynn?"

When I don't answer he keeps talking.

"Will you be OK here without me?"

No. No because I'm not OK here at all. No because I will never be OK here in Darkness with nothing I understand.

My knees shake. I thought I was going home.

I shrug again.

He crosses the floor, taking huge steps toward me. He's going to touch me. I gather my legs up on the side of the bed and scoot myself to the farther side.

He freezes. "Sorry," he mumbles.

He turns and crosses back to the door. "Charita's cooking some breakfast downstairs if you're hungry," he says. Then he's gone.

She's downstairs so I can't run away. She'd see me. And I don't remember the way anyway, so where would I go if I left?

I need to get out of here. I need a new plan.

* * *

Two days of eating and sitting and thinking.

I pull the chair in the Pink Stripes Room over to the window and I stare out of it and imagine Father Prophet coming up the road. He'll be in his pressed white pants with his white cape trailing behind him. His feet are so huge that his steps will make tremors in the road. The people on the other compounds, in the other houses, will rush out their doors as he passes and throw themselves on their knees at the curb of the road, begging him for mercy. He'll walk and he'll walk and her Light will be trailing behind him, brightening the street until it is burning all of the evil Liars. The little kids will follow him but he won't watch as they gather behind his cape. He'll keep walking, his eyes on my face through the glass, on me sitting here, waiting, until he's here, at the circle-y end of the road, underneath the window with his arms stretched toward me and that smile making his cheeks so large and then Mother God will make it so that I can float down to him on a beam of Light all because I remember.

Help me come up with a plan, Father. Help me get out of here. I believe in you.

I go downstairs to eat. Only to eat and steal food. My stomach gets so full from milk and pancakes and turkey and tacos and peanut butter and hamburgers and mac and cheese and bacon and guacamole and strawberries and ice cream and chicken and bread and a million other things that they eat in Darkness. I have to rub it to calm it down while I sit by the window or lie in the middle of all the pink stripes at night.

The plate under the bed piles up toward the mattress.

A smell gathers there, then spreads like fog between all of the pink stripes. The smell is good. The smell is food.

There's a pattern to the compound around me. I haven't figured out all of the pieces, all of the rules, but I can feel it. Louis knocks and says good-bye; Charita cooks a lot of food; Elsie leaves in a different car, then comes back; Junior is away a lot of the day; Elsie and Junior on the swing set; Jakey taking a nap; Elsie taking a nap; Elsie and Junior going away in a car, coming back. This is what I hear but they don't make me talk. They don't make me leave the window.

So I sit, I eat, I fail to come up with a plan.

Louis never takes me with him.

Then I'm two days closer to being thirteen. I only have seven days left.

Seven

THERE'S A KNOCKING ON MY DOOR. "Zylynn? You in there?"

I'm in here. I have been forever. I'm lying in my bed awake, staring at the ceiling and asking Father Prophet to give me a way out.

"Zylynn?" *Knock, knock.*

The voice is Charita's but it's so different from the voice she uses to quarrel with Louis. It's soft and almost like singing. The same voice she used when giving me peanut butter and strawberries. The same voice she used when holding Junior and Elsie and Jakey, all three of them on her one lap. It's weird that one woman can make her voice sound so different in the night than she does in the day.

"Zylynn?"

I don't want to answer her. I don't want to leave any more of my words out here. Father said that, even though we can't see them, to Mother God words are physical things. They're little pebbles made of Light. And if we leave them all over

Darkness, we leave little pebbles of our own Light out here, little parts of ourselves we can never get back.

"Get dressed, OK, Zylynn? Just wear the same clothes you've had on but with a new pair of underwear. We're going out," she says. "In the car."

Out. In the car. I sit up. Maybe Louis wasn't lying! Maybe they will take me home!

They want to send me back in brand-new underwear.

"OK," I say.

I get out of bed and take the soft clothes off my body. I put on the pale green underwear, the denim shorts. I button the pink buttons.

Father Prophet will make me throw all of these clothes away. He won't be happy with me now that it's my fourth day in Darkness. He'll be angry that I lost my white clothes. He'll want me to burn this pink shirt. I'll never tell him how much I like having a color against my skin. But he might know, just by looking at me.

Then I freeze with the shirt half buttoned. There will be a punishment. For leaving, even though the leaving was also my punishment. Father Prophet will say that if I wanted to stay badly enough, if I remembered him often enough, if I followed the rules closely enough, if I was sorry enough for that night, I would have stayed. I would have gotten back faster. There will be a punishment for the things that he'll know I liked: colors and food and softness and shampoo. Three days of silence. Two Hungry Days just for me. A pinging at the fence with all of the boys and girls throwing rocks at my legs. Maybe two punishments. Maybe all three at once.

I glance at the bottom of the bed where I've been stashing the plate. Maybe I should try to shove some strawberries or some bacon or that half peanut butter sandwich into the pocket of these shorts.

The door opens and Charita's head pops in. I whip my face around to see her. The yellow strap of a dress I've never seen is peeking through the door around her shoulder and her hair is down in flowing curls and her smile is huge and she looks like an entirely different person and I'm not prepared for it so I almost scream.

Her eyes go wide and her nose wrinkles. She makes a sound like a dog who has dirt stuck in his throat. "Zylynn," she says, "what's that sm—" Then she shakes her head. "Never mind. Glad you're up. Almost ready, kiddo?"

I'm so tired of being confused.

Forget the food. It doesn't matter. All that matters is that she'll take me back Inside. Relief floods my chest and limbs and I finish getting dressed.

A few minutes later, I'm in the car. It's me and Charita. I don't ask where Louis is. I don't ask why Louis is the one who got me but Charita is the one who's bringing me back. I don't ask if I can have my white shorts and T-shirt back so that Father isn't mad at me when I arrive. I don't ask any of these things, even though I want to. I've already left forty-nine words here in the Darkness, and I want to be able to tell

Father Prophet that I left fewer than fifty.

The car is not as scary in the daytime. The sunlight is slicing through the window, which is over our heads and baking the insides of the car even though there's air blowing on us through the openings in the front. Air-conditioning. We have that back at the compound, but we only turn it on on the very hottest days when Mother God is so angry she's trying to roast her creation back into ash.

The road moves too quickly under the tires and the turns make me want to yelp because they throw my body into the car door, but I won't. It's as fast and confusing and weird as it was on the way here, but it's not as scary. And that's because I know where I'm going. To safety. To the Light. Inside. In a few minutes or hours I will be back and I remember and Father might be mad about the clothes but he'll be happy that I remember. The Darkness didn't eat my brain. I still know Mother God. I still believe.

After a few days back Inside, after just a few days of breakfast and school and exercise and coming to the Light and dinner and prayers and bedtime, after only a few days of real life, I'll forget all about Louis and Charita and Elsie and Junior and Jakey and I will be like the rest of us who never ever left.

The best thing about being Inside—I've seen it happen with every new soul that the women gather—is that we forget all of the things Father Prophet didn't teach us. We forget the Darkness.

The best thing about Inside is not knowing anything else.

"Here, Zylynn. Breakfast," Charita says. She hands me a square with pink frosting. I lick it. It's so sweet my taste buds need to rearrange themselves before I should take a bite. I take one anyway. It squirts sweetness around my tongue and between my teeth and onto my inside-cheeks.

"Is that your first Pop-Tart?" Charita asks. She looks at me and it makes me nervous because she should be watching the road. I think that should be a rule out here.

I don't answer.

"Do you like it?" she asks.

I love it.

In the days before I forget, I will miss the food. But I still don't believe all the food can be real. It tastes real and it makes my stomach stick out in a real way. But it'll go away soon. It's a trick to keep me here, to make me addicted to Darkness.

I take another bite of Pop-Tart. I won't get addicted now. I don't need to worry. I'm going back.

The car slows down and I stuff another big bite into my mouth, trying to finish as much of it as I can before we stop and Father Prophet finds me again.

I remember you, I promise him. I hope he won't sense all the sugar in my mouth when he sees me.

The car stops and my heart speeds with the anticipation of Father Prophet's words and promises.

I look out the window but I don't see our compound. We're in a huge flat area made of gray concrete and full of cars.

Parking lot (n.): an area, usually divided into spaces, designed to store motor vehicles for long or short term

Charita gets out of the car. I shove in another bite.

Is this a different compound? Another land filled with things I've never heard of before and words I have to search for in the folds of my brain?

Find me. Please come find me.

Charita opens the door next to my seat.

"You coming?" she asks.

I don't answer.

"Come on," she says.

What if taking me "back" doesn't mean Inside. What if that wasn't what Louis meant at all? What if "back" is another compound, someplace worse than where I was, someplace where there isn't so much food and so many little kids who laugh all the time? And women? What if I failed a test and now comes the real punishment?

I stuff the rest of the Pop-Tart into my mouth. I should have shoved all of the food from the plate into the pockets of these shorts before we left.

I'm sorry I don't understand. What do I do? Father, I remember you.

Why aren't you answering me?

I'm frozen in the seat. Charita is staring at me.

"Are you OK, Zylynn?"

She's whispering: quiet and musical. I shake my head. A crumb escapes the corner of my mouth. I miss it immediately.

Charita squats by the car seat. She puts her hand on me and I don't want to like it there but I do. It's warm and soft and it looks like a tea-colored pillow on my pale knee.

"What's going on, Zylynn?"

"I'm sorry." I try to say it but it comes out all muffled.

"What?" Charita says.

"Please don't leave me here," I squeak through the Pop-Tart crumbs. "I'm sorry I've been bad."

Something invisible slashes across her face as if it's breaking open. Her brown eyes get bigger and her burgundy mouth turns into a circle and her arms come up until they're around me and her long black hair is hanging by my nose and it smells like oranges and she's holding me the way she held Junior and Elsie and Jakey and I realize that this is a hug and that, even though she's a woman, which means she carries all the pain and responsibility, the hug is for me and it's not for her and I feel my heart slow down because I've wondered for two days what a hug like this would feel like so I want to forget everything, every worry, every pain, and try to memorize it.

"You haven't been bad, Zylynn. You're not bad," Charita is whispering in my ear. "You're a good girl."

"Where are we?" I use my voice. I ask her because she's so close and because Father hasn't answered me.

"Target," she says.

Target (n.): an object, usually marked with concentric circles, to be aimed at during shooting practice or contests

I pull my head back to look at her. Maybe she's crazy.

"It's a store," she says. "Target is the name of a store. You need some more clothes. We only got you one outfit and three pairs of underwear."

> **Store** (n.): an establishment where merchandise is sold, usually on a retail basis

I need more clothes?

I don't understand anything here.

"Where we live, we wear different clothes every day." Charita finally gives me the first rule. She smiles at me. I feel mushy inside.

Hurry, Father, please. I'm starting to lose.

The glass doors slide open like magic and we step onto the bright white tile. I feel my pulse slow inside my skin. There are people everywhere, walking in all directions between the piles and piles of stuff in front of us. The people are pushing little carts, talking constantly like they don't know where they're going or what they're doing or how they're supposed to use their voices. There are some white walkways lining the place like guiding paths and between them there's nothing but stuff. Rows and piles, mountains and pits, shelves and buckets of stuff. Who needs all this stuff? Who are all these people?

I stand still as a stone with the artificial air freezing my skin and the sliding doors swishing back and forth behind me as more people push past me into this strange building. My eyes go wide, sucking it all in: the colors, the sounds, the smells.

It's overwhelming, but I'm calm. More calm than I've been in a while. Because over my head, miles and miles away, is a ceiling. And running along the ceiling, all over it from front to back and right to left and up to down are the brightest lights they have anywhere in Outside.

I stay like that for so long—enjoying the lights in my pupils—that I don't notice that Charita has left my side until she appears next to it again. She's pushing one of the red carts herself now, like she's one of the rest of these people.

They have dead eyes and faces that zoom this way and that, looking, looking, looking at the stuff but thinking about nothing.

"Who are all these people?" I ask her before it's too late to stop my voice from coming. But that's OK, actually, because I want to know. Are they from related compounds somehow? Do they say the same strange prayers that Elsie and Junior and Jakey say every night? How do they all know to come here, to Target? How do they all know what to do when they're here?

Charita says, "The shoppers?"

She says it with a question mark on the end, even though it's an answer. I will never understand things here.

I shouldn't be trying.

"Come on, *chiquita,*" Charita says.

I follow her over the white tiles—making sure to stay inside the two lines of red because that has to be what the rule is, even though Charita keeps breaking it by letting the back wheel cross into the red a little—and I watch the Shoppers. I see one woman standing frozen between two piles of T-shirts, tapping a pencil against a piece of paper. I see a small boy reach up from his perch in the red cart and throw a brightly colored flip-flop into it while the man pushing him around is looking in the other direction. I see a girl barely older than me holding up a skirt with pink sparkles and screaming at a nearby woman. I stare at her for a long time. This is what Father is always talking about: belongings, greed, Darkness. How can she live Outside and not even know she's in trouble?

Who are the Shoppers anyway?

Charita's cart comes to a sudden stop only about seven feet from the screaming girl.

She looks down at me, her brown eyes rimmed with eyelashes so black. I don't know how it's possible I haven't noticed them until now. "So?" she says.

My eyebrows jump a little.

Charita makes an arc with her hand, the silver band on her finger glinting under the glorious ceiling lights. "What do you like?" she asks.

I take a step back to see what she's looking at, but she seems to have pointed everywhere. To the shelves right next to us that are piled with neatly folded T-shirts in green and orange and brown and gray and stripes and flowers and dots. To the rack next to me where blue jeans hang in a straight line like they're waiting for their morning oatmeal. To the wall next to her where pastel flip-flops hang next to sunglasses and belts and purses. To the rack behind her where shiny patterned shirts are hung directly above poufy skirts and sequined shorts.

I see now that the Shoppers have some order to all of the stuff. It isn't in piles and pits the way it first looked. Everything is lined up like it has a place, like there are some rules and once I learn them maybe I can survive. Until I figure out a way to get home.

I look up, debating whether it's worth it to use my voice to answer Charita's question, but then she opens her mouth and changes it. "Zylynn," she says softly, like she did a minute ago at the car. Or maybe even softer. She says my name so softly it makes something light up in my brain. It makes me think something I've never thought about anyone before: *she likes me*. "What do you want?"

A chill goes down my spine. The goose bumps on my arms are no longer from the air-conditioning.

"What do I want?" I repeat, hushed. This has to be a trick. I know it's a trick. But I also believe her eyes and her voice and they don't want to trick me.

She nods. "Don't go crazy," she says.

I'm not, I think. But then I wonder if I am, maybe.

"But pick out a few shirts, maybe five. And three pairs of shorts or skirts. Whatever you like. Everything here is about as affordable as we're going to get."

Index cards flip in my brain.

Affordable (adj.): believed to be within one's financial means

I still don't know what she's talking about.

"I'm sorry that we can't buy more for you right now. We only have so much set aside. But we'll get a small wardrobe going for the summer, and then we'll do a big shopping spree with all the kids before school starts . . ."

I stare at her, not hearing. "I can have whatever T-shirt I want?" What kind of rule is that?

Charita nods. I see something breaking in her eyes. I wonder if the lies are breaking; if she likes me enough, maybe she won't be able to lie anymore.

I wander to the shelf of T-shirts behind her. I touch a yellow one, pale, like the sun in the winter. I run my finger over it. I've never touched yellow.

It feels like the rest of Outside: soft.

Soon, the shirt is on my body. I'm standing in a tiny room full of mirrors. It's in a hallway full of other tiny rooms full of mirrors. Charita led me in here, piled the stuff on the bench, and instructed me to put on one of the outfits so we can "see if it fits."

I have on the yellow shirt and a pair of jeans that only reach right below my knees. Not quite pants and not quite shorts. Charita called them "capris."

"How's it going in there?" she shouts over the doorway. The door doesn't reach the ceiling in this little room. It also doesn't reach the floor. So she left me alone in here, but I can see her shoes poking out the bottom of the door. I can tell she's guarding me, keeping me trapped so I won't run.

I don't answer.

After a few minutes she says, "Zylynn, honey, want to let me in so I can see if the clothes fit?"

I open the door and she comes in. She reaches for my waist, which makes me jump.

"Sorry, sorry," she says. "Lift your shirt so I can see the waistline, OK? I won't touch you ever if you don't want me to."

I lift the shirt. All of these rules are coming so fast now, I don't have time to think about them before I'm following them.

"Hmm," Charita says. She taps a finger on her chin. "Those look a little baggy on you, don't they? Why don't you put on the tan shorts while I go and see if I can find them a size smaller. Would that be OK?"

My eyes go wide. I can hardly believe it. She's going to leave me.

I nod.

"OK," she says, "I'll be right back."

I listen to her shoes slapping the soles of her feet until she turns out of the hallway of rooms and then she's gone.

She said to put on a new pair of shorts, but I don't have to. I don't have to follow her rules. She's not the Prophet.

Instead I tiptoe down the hallway myself and out into the bright lights again. I spot Charita, the back of her dark curls as she's bent over a shelf holding all sorts of jeans. But she can't see me.

I turn the other way, tiptoe tiptoe tiptoe, until I'm in the middle of a whole new bunch of stuff, stuff we haven't seen yet, and I'm sure she won't be able to find me.

It's my chance. I have to run. I'll figure out the way home once I get out of here. Father will help me find it. I'll run and run until I find that shrugging cactus. *I'm on my way, Father.*

I look around, but I don't see the door. I have to get through the door, into the parking lot, through all of the cars, and out onto the road.

I stand between two metal racks full of heavy, dark-colored dresses and look right and left, left and right. I can't find the door. All of the walls feel miles and miles away from these dresses.

There's a woman with a cart only about five feet away from me. She's a Liar too because she's here and she's a Shopper and she's not a Child Inside the Light. She's walking toward me, close, closer, closer.

I can't let her see me. I can't let her talk to me.

I dive between two of the dresses on the rack to the left and then I'm in a little dress-cave. They surround me with their colors. It's too close to dark in here. But it's the only place I can go. There's another woman out there now. There are legs all around me.

I take two of the dresses in my hand and peek out. Where is the door? Where is the door?

Please, Father. Help me. Help me get home.

And that's when I see it. A big sign, close to the ceiling. Exit.

Exit (n.): a way or passage out

Father put a whole sign up there just for me.

I hold my breath until the strangers' legs are gone, and then I dart out between two of the dresses and I run. I'm wearing the yellow T-shirt and the silly capris. I don't have shoes on. But I don't care. This is my chance. I run fast, fast, fast as I can toward Exit.

Sock, sock, sock, sock, sock.

My socks want to slide on the tiled floor but I won't let them. I lift my feet up too quickly for them to slip. I'm running so fast my feet maybe don't touch the floor.

I haven't run this fast since that night. The bad night. The Abomination.

There are Shoppers everywhere but I can't worry about them. I dart past them. Maybe I run so fast they can't see me.

And then I see the door. It's there. In front of me. I can make it. It's closer than the showers are to the Girls' Dorm. It's closer than the Dining Hall is to the Boys' Dorm. I can make it.

CRASH.

I run right into one of the Shoppers and fall down on my

butt. He's a huge man, bigger than any on the compound, and he's dressed entirely in blue with little shiny metal things stuck on his shirt.

"Where you going, young lady?" he says.

But I don't have to answer him. He's not the Prophet.

I stand and look at him like I'm going to answer. He sticks a fat hip out, leaning to the left. That's it. I break to the right of him and—*whoosh*—I'm past him! I'm getting out of here.

But then I freeze. I see someone—a girl—going through the door. It's—

That girl's hair is long, but hers would be longer now. It's spiky and pushed off her head in all sorts of directions. And the girl is not wearing white. She's wearing a hot-pink shirt. And she's not with any of the Brothers. She's with a whole bunch of other girls her age.

But all that could happen in Darkness . . . I think it's—

Just before she goes through the door, I see her throw her head back like she's laughing. And I'm sure.

"Jaycia!" I yell.

I take another step, trying to get to her. If I can find her, I can get all the way home. Jaycia knows everything. She'll know the way.

"Jaycia!" I scream, but she's almost through the door.

Big hands come down hard on my shoulders and I'm lifted into the air.

"We don't take too kindly on kids running off in our clothes, little girl," the Man in Blue says.

The girl who might have been Jaycia disappears through the door.

And I have a Liar touching me. It should burn. It will burn. If he holds me for another second my shoulders will catch on fire.

"Where's your mother?" he asks.

My mother is God.

It had been a feast day, so I wasn't hungry. But the orange was in my right hand anyway. The banana was in my left hand.

"It's OK, Zylynn," Thesmerelda said. "Take it."

It was night. The dorm around me was sleeping. Thesmerelda had come into our dorm and climbed the ladder next to the bed where I slept. She'd woken me with a palm stroking my hair.

It felt weird. I wasn't used to touching yet. The women had just come back that afternoon.

It was a long time ago. Before Jaycia came. Before I was in charge of the Girls' Dorm. Before I slept in the top bunks like the oldest girls. I was in a middle bunk.

"But I'm not hungry," I said.

Thesmerelda smiled. "Good," she said. Her hair was long past her shoulders, striped with blond and gray. Her skin was so pale all of the lights on the walls reflected off it. "It's good not to be hungry," she said. "You take these, OK? You put them under your covers. You keep them here for the next Hungry Day."

I was getting scared. No one had ever handed just one of us food before. We all got food together.

"It's all right, Zylynn," Thesmerelda said, smiling. "I asked Father and he said I could give these to you. He said Mother was very pleased with you. I'm only delivering her prizes."

Now I smiled. I was good. So good Mother God found a way to deliver me two pieces of fruit.

"Go back to sleep now, OK, child?" Thesmerelda said. "It is right and perfect to sleep through the dark night. Drink some tea."

I nodded. I drank some tea and put my head on the pillow. Thesmerelda stroked my clumpy hair until I was asleep.

When Brother Zascays came to wake us in the morning, I thought maybe it was a dream. But no, I still had the orange and the banana.

And that day was a Hungry Day.

The Man in Blue puts me in a little room and tries to get me to tell him my name. I stand in a corner and shake.

He's getting ready to punish me. I know it. I'm not sure which of the Shoppers's rules I broke, but I broke one. Or two. Or more. And punishments in Darkness have to be worse than Inside.

"What's your name, little girl?" he says again. "I have to get ahold of your mother so that I can let you go."

I stare at the light in the ceiling. She's here, I remind myself. She's everywhere. My mother.

Please help me, Father.

And then Charita is in the doorway. "Zylynn!" she gasps. "I was so worried. I was—don't do that to me, OK? Don't run away. Don't hide. If you need something, we'll work it out. You don't have to run."

I'm still shaking. I'm ready for her to hit me. For Charita and the Man in Blue to put me up against a fence and have the other Shoppers throw rocks at my legs and my back. For something so much worse I can't imagine it.

Instead she rushes at me and gathers me into her arms again. I let her. A hug is better than a punishment.

"She didn't know what she was doing, sir. Can't you see that?" Charita says over my head. Then she pulls back to look at me.

"Where did you go? What were you doing?"

If she realizes I was running away, she'll never let me out of her sight. I'll never be able to get out of here. So I say the first thing I can think of.

"I thought I saw Jaycia," I say.

"Who's Jaycia?" Charita asks.

"Someone I know. From . . . home . . . before."

"From the compound?" Charita asks.

I nod.

"Where was she?" Charita asks. "Did you talk to her?"

"Going through the door," I say. "No."

"Oh, sweetie," Charita says. She strokes my head. "I don't think you saw her. I think you're so homesick you really, really wanted to see her. And then your brain tricked you into thinking you did. Is that possible?"

I shrug.

Yes, it's possible. In fact, it couldn't have been her. The girl I saw going through the door was laughing. That girl was happy. That girl was fine.

And Jaycia is doomed.

I wish they would give me my punishment. It's too awful to wait and wait and wait for it.

"OK," the Man in Blue says. "I'll let you two go."

"Come on," Charita says. "Let's go home. We can try on the rest of everything there."

I stare at them for a long time before I stand up. I wait for them to trick me. I hold my breath. But the punishment never comes.

These are the things in the cart: the pair of blue jean capris, a pair of white shorts, a pair of gray shorts, a purple shirt that buttons up like my pink one, a gray T-shirt, a white T-shirt, a blue tank top, a red tank top, a pink tank top, two more packages of brightly colored underwear for me and one for Elsie (because she's running out; I don't know what that means), two packages of white socks, green flip-flops, brown sunglasses, and the yellow T-shirt that's the color of the winter sun.

It's more than Charita first listed but she keeps saying, "It's OK. You need it."

I don't know what I need it for. I don't know the rules. But the rules say they aren't going to starve me or beat me for following the girl I thought was Jaycia. And the rules say all of this is mine.

I won't think about how wobbly that makes me feel.

We stand in a long line of other people and other full carts as the lady behind the counter takes turns beeping each piece of stuff against a machine.

I'm safe for now. Charita doesn't know I tried to run away. Charita wants to give me softness and colors. So I won't let the wobbly feeling crawl all the way into me as we stand in this line and it inches closer and closer to the beeping. I'll save the guilt for later, for at Charita's house when Father Prophet might be coming to find me and punish me since I didn't follow his Exit sign.

Toward the front of the line we're between two more sets of shelves. On our left there's a tiny refrigerator with a see-through window that's full of soda bottles standing up like they're begging you to take them and then rows and rows and rows of brightly colored bags of food. On our right are shelves and shelves of things I've never seen before.

The little kid who's sitting in the cart ahead of us reaches his hand out and pulls a bright green plastic turtle off the shelf. He pulls on its arm and it goes up and down. "Bye-bye, Target," he says in a silly low voice.

The woman at the front of the cart snatches it out of his hand. "We're not getting that, Gregory!" she says. "You have plenty to play with at home."

I watch her put the turtle back on the shelf. Gregory screams and cries and I stare at the plastic turtle.

I've only seen a picture of a turtle once on one of the classroom computers. I've never seen one for real or in plastic.

"Zylynn?" Charita says. I snap out of it and find her staring at me. "Do you want that?" she asks.

"What is it?" I say.

She laughs. "It's a toy."

> **Toy** (n.): an object, often a small representation of something familiar, for children to play with; a plaything

I bite my lips and shake my head.

But she puts it in the cart anyway.

"We live in the evil state of America," Father Prophet said in Chapel.

We sat on the stone benches. They were hard and cold and uncomfortable but we were trying to listen. If we were uncomfortable, it meant Mother God was not pleased. It was our fault.

Jaycia was sitting next to me. Too close. It was a Mistake to sit too close. I wondered if that's why the benches felt so cold and hard.

But I didn't move away. She was doing this thing with her

voice, so quiet that only I could hear. It went up and down and up and down in a mmmm sound. Humming.

"You belong to the Light," Father said.

We all applauded. We kissed the air. That was a joyful sentence.

"Yes, it is a good thing. It is a very good thing. But the hardest part about belonging to the Light is the belonging. You belong to her. Nothing belongs to you."

We nodded. We heard this all the time.

"We live in a greedy state. The people in Darkness, and you, you who are still addicted to whatever degree, you who are still battling that sneaky demon Curiosity, you think you can have your own. My own bed. My own thought. My own child."

We nodded like we were supposed to.

"Greed is the beginning of all evil. Without belongings, no country would own bombs for war; no human would own guns with which to destroy other humans; no one would steal or pillage or kidnap. There would be no drugs, no violence, no Darkness. So why do we want our belongings so fiercely? Why do the people of Darkness hold on so tightly to their money, their cars, their . . . what's the worst thing you can own?"

He made a face like he would throw up.

"Guns," we said.

Father Prophet smiled a half smile and nodded. "You won't be like the people of Darkness. You must give up your desire to own. You must strike the word 'mine' from your lips. You belong to the Light. You belong to Her.

"And why, why, why do so many humans choose belongings and Darkness over the Light?"

We shifted in our seats. We knew the answer. This was a standard talk, one he'd give once a week or month or something. Jaycia leaned closer to me. It made me wonder if she'd heard it before.

It made me wonder if she had belongings back in the Darkness. If it was hard for her to give belongings up. If she had greed.

But I tried to stop wondering because wondering is bad.

"Greed. Only the Light frees you from greed. All good things come from Light and all bad things come from greed. You have nothing, you own nothing, you are free to be owned by our Mother. And you reach her through me."

Nine

I'M LYING ON THE BED IN the Pink Stripes Room surrounded by plastic bags with red circles printed on them. When I roll over or move my leg I hear the crinkling of plastic against the fabric inside. The fabrics that are soft and cozy and light and breezy and pink and red and yellow and gray and white. The fabrics Charita said are for me.

It's a lie. I know it. The food under my bed. The clothes on top of it. The fact that I just thought of this bed as mine.

I can't have belongings. I have to remember that. It's getting harder and harder to remember everything.

But I'm talking to Father Prophet. Praying. I'm telling him that I remember always. I remember my Abomination. I remember that he said it was my choice to stay here, that if I really want to, I'll find a way out. I remember his white clothes and his cropped gray hair and his darting gray eyes. I remember the feasts when the women came home and the pain of Hungry Days and pingings at the fence when we needed to be punished. I remember the mushy oatmeal and how great it tasted the day after a Hungry Day. I remember the buzzing lights and bedtime prayers and all of the rules.

I'm talking to Father Prophet but I'm talking for myself. I'm listing everything I remember from School and Exercise and Chapel, from the kids and the men and the women, from the whitewashed buildings (seven in the first circle, ten or more in the second circle, more more more in the third circle), and the clay paths that spread like spiderwebs in the center of all the circles, and so so so much Light.

Father Prophet made it seem so easy—Remember the Light and you'll be here when you turn thirteen. Remember the Light and you have nothing to worry about.

But how do I get home when I don't know the way? Why did that big Liar in the blue clothes have to stop me? If I'd only reached Jaycia, I'd be on the way home now.

Except that wasn't Jaycia. That girl was smiling and laughing. And Jaycia is doomed. She's stuck in the Darkness forever. She's being starved and beaten and punished and burned. Exactly like I will be if I don't run away.

Because I did the same bad thing Jaycia did.

"Zylynn." I hear Charita's voice call from below the pink stripes. "Come down for lunch!"

I keep forgetting that lunch happens every day here.

"This is a new decree," Father Prophet said.

There was a wiggling of excitement through the Chapel, a straightening of spines, an opening of ears.

I was being held against a larger body. I was small, tiny.

My head was on a chest and my arms were draped around a pair of huge shoulders and my eyelids were heavy. "Don't fall asleep," a soft voice kept whispering in my ear. "You can't fall asleep in Chapel, Zy-Zy. Father will get angry."

I strained to keep my eyes open.

We were sitting on stone benches and in front of us Father Prophet stood on the small red stage with the scratchy floor. He wore bright-white pants with a certain crease in the front of each leg. He wore a white T-shirt and a white cape was draped over his shoulders. His hair was brown and his face was round and mushy like if I stuck my finger into it, it would hold that shape. His eyes were gray.

He closed them and began to mumble under his breath. *"Hem in ay ah. Hem in ay ah. Hem in ay ah."* The sound was rhythmic and soft in my ears and I felt my eyelashes flutter against the neck of the body that was holding me.

"Open those eyes, Zy-baby," he said, barely audible. "Listen to the Father."

Father Prophet's voice boomed against the stone benches and the stone walls and the ceiling with its oblong lights running across it. "Mother God is here! Let us be grateful for her presence."

We jolted upright. We kissed the air to show our love for the Creator of Light.

"Have we pleased you, Mother God? Have we been good Children?"

We held a breath, waiting for her answer. Her answer would determine everything about the coming week: how much food we would eat, how often we'd get to be outdoors, who would stay and who would go.

"Hem in ay ah. Hem in ay ah. Hem in ay ah."

Now I was awake. My little heart beat against my little rib cage, my little brain eager to soak up whatever new words or teaching Mother God had for us today.

With a whoosh of his breath and his cape, Father Prophet stopped chanting. He almost seemed to deflate to normal height and normal eyes.

"She is not happy," he said.

The big people all around muttered immediately: "Mother of Light, Mother of Light, we are sorry. Mother of Light, Mother of Light, we deserve nothing. Mother of Light . . ." The Act of Contrition. I was too small to know it back then, though.

"SILENCE!" Father Prophet belted.

Silence.

"She says we are bothering her," he said.

We rattled with surprise. We sucked in air.

"She says there are too many small requests every day. She's getting tired, weary."

He squished his gray eyes closed again.

"What shall we do?" he asked.

I felt the body I was braced against deflate. I felt the entire room deflate. The energy zapped from body to body to body: worry, fear, guilt, shame. We all felt the same things like we were supposed to.

"It is not your fault," Father said. "I told you to pray to her. But how could you know what to pray? You all come from

Darkness. You all work ceaselessly to cast the dark ways far from your souls. You cannot be expected to pray perfectly."

There was nodding now, mumbles of agreement. Relief.

I was awake, staring at the stubbly chin of the person who was holding me. I was confused.

"I will fix it," Father said.

We erupted into calls of "Thank you, Father" and "Yes, yes" and "I believe, we believe" and "Praise the Light."

"Say your bedtime prayer," he said when we calmed down. "Say your morning prayers, say the standard prayers that you have learned, that you have been taught here Inside. Say only the prayer that you have perfected through me.

"But do not use your own prayer. If you have a specific need that you think is deserving of Mother God's time and attention, you must bring it to me. First. And I will present your need to Mother God, Creator of Light."

I felt the body that was holding me go stiff. I saw the green eyes in his head go angry. From the bodies around me there was still relief, thanks, praise. But something was not right with the arms clasping me close.

"Do not speak directly to Mother God in your own words," Father Prophet concluded. "I will bear that burden for you. I will be your voice. I will take your prayers to our Mother perfectly. And she will always answer me."

"Zylynn," Charita says from behind my head as I sit again at the table in their little kitchen. "Do you like turkey?"

Her words shake the memory from my brain leaving me

only with questions. *Was it Louis holding me so many years ago? Was he really there? Why can I remember this now?*

"Zylynn? Turkey?" Charita repeats.

I shake my head to clear the questions. I have to find a way home. I can't let Curiosity get into my brain now.

"Is that a no?" Charita asks. "You don't like turkey?"

They must be stupid here, in Darkness, because they haven't figured out that I don't want to talk. That I won't if I can help it. And, of course, everyone likes turkey. It's meat. A delicacy. But I know whatever they will give me, turkey or peanut butter or strawberries or Pop-Tarts, I know it's a lie. They can't figure out what I know.

I'm angrier at Charita now that we're back on her compound with all of those lies piled on my bed. She made me like the clothes. But I won't believe in them. I know that as soon as the Darkness addicts me, the clothes and food and hugs and smiles will all disappear.

"Turkey, Zylynn?" she says again.

I chew the inside of my cheek.

Across the table Junior and Jakey stare at me with those bright green eyes like they think I'll answer. I feel sorry for them, for never having a chance.

But eventually the Gatherers will come for them. Eventually they'll learn the truth and get to choose between Light and greed. Everyone gets the choice at some point. That's what Father Prophet said.

Even though some of the Children Inside the Light choose to turn back to Darkness. Some choose to become Liars all over again. Did Louis do that? Why would anyone do that?

A little hand tugs at my elbow. I turn and there's Elsie. Her hair is in braids again today and her smile reveals a row of white teeth divided with huge gaps. "I like turkey," she says. "Do you?"

When she talks to me, it's different, right? She's not an Agent of Darkness. She's too small.

"Everyone likes turkey," I say.

She smiles.

I have a feeling inside my chest, a lightness, almost like its own little smile. I have a feeling like I put that smile there on Elsie's face.

It's nighttime again. I say my Bedtime Prayer under the lightbulb and lie down on the bed. I kick the plastic bags to the floor hoping that the crinkling sound will escape from between the pink stripes and somehow remind Louis of what he said a few nights ago. Make him take me back.

I beg for a way home all day every day and I'm still here.

It feels unfair. It feels like Louis broke a promise even though I only heard him say it through the pink stripes in the first place. And even though he's a Liar and I can't trust anything he says.

It's been four days.

Now there are two plates of food under my bed, brimming over. I only took a few bites at dinner tonight; my stomach is full, so full it aches. My belly button was pushing out toward the mirror on the wall when I looked. I didn't know a stomach could get this full off actual food, not just water.

But I have to stop thinking about food and smiles and hugs.

Tomorrow there will only be six days before my thirteenth birthday. I cannot believe I already failed for four straight days. I need to spend every second remembering Father Prophet so that he will give me a way to escape.

I close my eyes and try to see his face. The gray, darting eyes. The white collar around his neck. The gray hair so short it would tickle our palms if he was in a good mood and let us touch it. The stubbly cheeks that hung off his eye sockets and jaw in excess.

I remember all of those things about it, but when I try to put them together, to make a picture of his face in my brain it doesn't happen. It gets mixed up with Louis's ears and Junior's eyes and Elsie's smile.

No! Think! I tell myself. *Father Prophet.*

I shake my head to erase all of the other colors and faces and thoughts. I concentrate on his crooked nose, lumpy forehead, large waist, creased white pants.

He's not there. Only pieces of him are floating around in my head. I can't make my brain put the puzzle together.

My heart speeds up and my breath catches. I've forgotten him already. In only a few days. I can't picture him anymore.

Father, Father, Father, I plead. Help me.

Nothing happens. Nothing has been happening. I keep

talking to him but I'm still here in Darkness and hearing nothing. Why won't he come?

Now I'm close to angry, which has to be worse than simple forgetting. Now I'm close to panic, which is the opposite of trust.

Who can I turn to if Father is gone?

What would happen if . . . ?

It's Curiosity making me do it. A little Curiosity mixed in with good things like desperation and despair. For the first time in my life, I turn in the wrong direction.

Mother God, Creator of Light, I don't mean to bother you with this, but I need to get back into your Light. Will you please help Father Prophet find me?

Will you please protect me from the Darkness?

The light above my head flicks brighter, dimmer, brighter, dimmer, brighter, dimmer.

If Father Prophet can't hear me, at least she can.

Still, I feel guilty as I fall into sleep.

Jen

THE KNOCK ON THE PINK STRIPES Room door the next morning is not click-y and full of fingernails. It's not rough and low like Louis's either. It's a bouncy little sound that seems too small for knuckles.

I turn to look at the closed door, but I don't say anything. I said too many words yesterday.

I'm sitting at the window again, staring out of it and down the street toward Inside but I'm not picturing Father Prophet sweeping me up in a laser of light. I'm trying, but I can't quite remember his face, or the way his hand felt when he patted the top of my head, or the way his voice bounced off the stone benches in Chapel.

Will he be mad at me for praying to Mother God? It felt like I couldn't reach him; but what if I didn't try hard enough? What if praying to Mother God means I'll never get back Inside? Or my punishment will be even worse than a Hungry Day or a pinging or standing between the boards?

The worst punishment yet?

But Mother God is the Creator of Light and order and everything good. She's supposed to love me. So how could she punish me forever? As long as I get back to her, she won't punish me forever. But if I'm stuck out here . . .

Bonk, bonk, bonk.

The knocking on the door continues.

I look down at my feet. I'm wearing the green flip-flops, the blue jean capris, the yellow T-shirt. I'm wrapped in a rainbow. My heart squeezes between the prongs of my ribs when I think about how fun it was to dress myself this morning. But the guilt is little; it's smaller than it was yesterday or any day before.

And the parts of me where the guilt is gone are filled up to the top with something else: sadness. Loneliness.

With one final bonk the door inches open. It creaks behind my head.

"Zylynn?" says Elsie's squeaky voice. Her head sneaks around the white door, one braid swinging toward the floor. She fuses her eyes on me.

I nod.

She's smiling so huge it's like a pinprick to my heart.

She scurries across the gold carpet coming closer and closer to me and I think about hiding against the wall like I would if Louis were approaching, but I don't because she's so small or because her smile is so big or because of what happened yesterday when I told her I like turkey. I'm not afraid of her.

She bounces over the bed and drops to sitting at my feet.

"Cool!" she says, too loudly. "What is that?"

She points to my lap. In it is the turtle. Even though it's plastic, it feels warm and happy on my leg, like a stone that's been in the sun all day.

I don't want to let it go, but I hand it to her.

"Cool," she says again, in a hushed whisper. I wonder if cool and warm are opposites Outside. She turns it over in her hand, studying it, then stands it up on the floor and makes one of its legs go back and forth. "Hiyaaah! Hiyah!" she says. "I'm kicking all the bad guys, see, Zylynn?"

I look at her on my carpet, smiling at me.

Could this be why Father Prophet let them take me? Is Elsie my reason? If I bring her back, will I finally be forgiven for my Abomination? Do I need to do something that huge to make up for the most awful thing I ever did?

"Did Mom get him for you while we were at camp yesterday?" she asks.

I nod. "Mom" is what they call Charita. They call Louis "Dad," like he said. When they say they're going to "camp" it means they aren't here in the house or on the compound. It's confusing. I don't know why everyone can't go by their names and stay where they're supposed to be.

"Hiyah!" she says again, with another fake kick. Then she looks up at me and her eyes are so wide and so green and so much like mine. I want to sit on the floor with another plastic turtle and let her pretend to kick it. "It's so cool that you share," she says.

Share (v.): to divide and distribute, apportion

My heart shakes in my chest. I do not want her to divide my turtle.

My turtle. Is it really mine? My pulse is like the loudest wind ever in my ears. My heart hangs—heavy, guilty—close to my stomach.

"I always wanted a sister," she goes on.

I flip for the word but it isn't there. She's looking at me like *sister* is me, even though I was already *daughter*. It's all so confusing and I only want to be *Zylynn*.

Actually, not even that. I only want to be a part of the Light.

But with my turtle.

Elsie holds the turtle toward me, the yellow part of his shell first so that I can see his face, and his arms look like they're reaching out to grab my hand. "What's his name?" she asks.

I tilt my head.

"He's cute," she says. "What's his name?"

Her smile finally makes me use my voice. "I don't know." Do turtles have names?

She giggles. How can she do that so easily? "He's your turtle," she says. "You should give him a name."

My turtle.

"I should?"

Elsie nods. "What do you want to call him?"

I shrug. She smiles at me for so long I can't keep my mouth still. "Turtle," I say finally.

She giggles again, nodding. "Turtle," she says. "Can Turtle sit between us at breakfast?"

"I don't know." How would I know? How does she expect me to know these things?

I feel a strange pinch in my cheeks, an ache in my jaw. I move my fingers to my lips and that's when I realize it: I'm smiling too.

There's a bang behind us. We both jump. When I turn, Louis is standing on the other side of the open door, coughing and wiping his eyes.

"Daddy!" Elsie squeals. In an instant she's back across the room and has climbed onto his hip like he's not an Agent of Darkness at all. I brace myself to save her if I have to.

"Meet Turtle," she says, shoving the toy into his wet face.

"I'm heading to work, girls. You keep playing, OK?"

> **Play** (v.): to exercise or employ oneself in amusement; to engage in a game alone or with others

Elsie squeezes the Liar's neck in a hug and I wonder: *playing*. Is that what we were doing?

Back at home, after breakfast, we will all go to school. Well, all of us except me.

Our first class is Computers, then we start Outside Studies. We will sit in rows: oldest girls in the front, then oldest boys, medium girls, then medium boys, small girls, small boys. The

Teacher will walk between the aisles, his feet shifting over the sand. He'll yell a new word.

"Turtle!"

And we'll chant the answer. "Any reptile of the order Testudines, comprising aquatic and terrestrial species having the trunk enclosed in a shell consisting of a dorsal carapace and a ventral plastron."

Or he'll yell a word we learned years and months ago. It might be new for the littles or the mediums. "Helicopter!"

And we'll chant the answer. "Any of a class of heavier-than-air craft that are lifted and sustained in the air horizontally by rotating wings or blades turning on vertical axles through power supplied by an engine."

Sometimes one of us will get it wrong and that one will have to stand between the painted wooden poles with our back pressed too tight against one of them until class is over and there's a blue streak painted next to our spine. The only color we ever wear on our clothes. Shame.

Unless there's a stranger in the classroom. Sometimes there are strangers. They started showing up months or a year ago. Recently. A man or a woman dressed in black with a jacket on, even when there's no air-conditioning in the classroom. The strangers never say anything to us. They sit in the back and take notes.

There was a stranger there when Hermeel got the answer to "helicopter" wrong. He stood. He was walking toward the Boards of Shame to press his back against them.

And Brother Manamak said, "Sit, Hermeel." We didn't know why. He got the answer wrong. He was not supposed to sit. But Hermeel sat. The stranger's pen went scratch-scratch-scratch on this board thing she was carrying around.

Hermeel didn't get punished until later. Until after she left. He didn't get the Boards of Shame, he got a pinging instead. He stood with his nose pressed to the fence, as close to Outside as he could be while he was still in the Light. And we stood a few feet away from him. I didn't like pinging him with those rocks that day. I didn't like flinging the rocks so they would hit his legs and back. Usually the pingings are fun. Usually they're Mother God's way of using us to get her justice. Usually we squeal with delight when we get a direct ping.

But that day it was confusing. I didn't understand how Hermeel had broken the rules.

Playing is not hard. I don't even have to talk. Elsie takes Turtle all around the Pink Stripes Room. She walks over to the bed and puts Turtle tummy down on the blanket, swishing him back and forth.

"Look, Zylynn!" she says. "He's swimming."

I nod.

She runs over to the desk and bounces Turtle up and down on his legs. "Look, Zylynn!" she says, "he's dancing."

I nod. It's all I have to do.

My cheeks still hurt. Elsie's smile is making them pinch.

"Elsie!" Charita's voice comes flying up the stairs. "Elsie!

Get down here! You have to eat before camp!"

Elsie bounces over to where I still sit in the chair. She puts her mouth too close to my ear and blows into it in a "Shhh."

My shoulder comes up to scratch at my ear. Her voice itches being that close.

"It won't matter if I don't eat before camp," she says.

My eyes go wide. She doesn't want to eat?

"Zylynn?" Charita's voice comes up the stairs again, a little quieter, a little more of a question. "Would you like to come down for breakfast?"

"Nope," Elsie whispers but I don't know why. She says it too quietly for Charita to hear from all the way downstairs. Elsie is standing at the desk still, making Turtle spin on his shell.

I stand and walk out of the room. Playing was all right but eating is better. Elsie follows me down the stairs anyway.

I sit at the table in the spot that has been assigned to me. Junior's already eating and Jakey's smashing banana slices into his ears in his high chair. Scrambled eggs and strawberries appear under my nose like magic. This place is magic. I'm starting to wish the food would disappear so I could figure out the tricks and make myself want all the way to go home.

I almost spit out my first bite of eggs.

I do want to go home. All the way.

Elsie sits next to me and puts Turtle at the top of my plate. "Here," she says. "Here's Turtle, Zylynn."

Charita spins around from the stove and stares. "What

were you two doing?" she asks.

Elsie shrugs. "Playing," she says.

"You were?" Charita asks.

Elsie nods.

"You two? Together?" Charita asks.

Elsie nods again. She takes a bite of eggs.

"Wow," Charita says.

She's still smiling at me when I finish my last bite.

I stare out the window until lunch. I watch Father Prophet come up the road like usual: the light, the cape, the people bowing on the curbs, the little children following, the way he looks at me. I'm almost remembering his face.

I have to remember it before I can go home. Once I know his face, he'll give me a plan.

Boom. The front door slams below me. I listen. Someone or someones who is not Louis or Charita or Jakey or Elsie or Junior comes to the front door and makes a lot of noise until Junior and Elsie go out the door with them. Charita says, "Thank you so much," to the someone/someones. Jakey and Charita stay in the kitchen. He shouts and talks and squeals. She clanks dishes together. Then they come upstairs and go into a room that is not the Pink Stripes Room that I'm in and is not the room next to the Pink Stripes Room where Louis and Charita had a quarrel. Then Jakey gets quiet and Charita goes back downstairs by herself and it makes me queasy to think that there are three people in this house and for some reason they're all in three totally separate places.

I look for Father Prophet again. He's not there. *Where are you?*

I try the playing thing. I get up and walk to the desk. I put Turtle on his shell and spin. I do it again. My eyes watch him spin around and around until if he were a real turtle he'd be so dizzy. It's sort of nice to watch him, but my cheeks don't pinch like they did before. I'm no good at playing.

I put him in my pocket and I go downstairs. Even though no one told me to.

Mistake? Abomination?

"Zylynn," Jaycia hissed into the lightbulb hanging between our beds. It was night, middle of the night. It was after a Hungry Day.

"Shh," I said. I was supposed to stop the whispering. Whispering was a Mistake. Even if I wanted to hear her laugh again, I couldn't let her. We had to do the right thing always.

"Zylynn," she said. She didn't sound like she was going to laugh.

"You have to be quiet," I told her.

Her head popped up in the bed next to mine. The lights had to sneak around her. She was a shadow in the dorm.

"I had a nightmare," she said.

Oh. We could speak when someone had nightmares. I don't know why. I didn't know why the rules were the rules and I didn't wonder, then. Curiosity stayed far away from Mother God's home.

I got out of bed and climbed the rope ladder next to hers. I patted her head. "There there," I said.

She lowered her eyebrows. "What are you doing?" she asked.

I was doing what I was supposed to because I was the one in charge.

"Stopping the nightmare," I said. It was usually only the littlest girls who had nightmares. Or the newest girls. And the nightmares were always loud; they woke me up. And when I found the girl being loud, she was always still asleep. I was supposed to pat her until her eyes opened, then give her some more pomegranate tea.

I didn't know what to do with Jaycia. She was awake already.

"It won't stop unless I eat," she said.

All of our stomachs grumbled to echo her. They clenched and spread and clenched and spread in pain.

"Do you have an orange under your covers?" I asked. My orange and banana were long gone. Thesmerelda hadn't been back to give me more fruit either.

"What? No," Jaycia said. "What are you talking about?"

My face burned and I didn't answer. She hadn't said so, but I thought maybe the orange and the banana were a secret, just between me and Thesmerelda and Father Prophet and Mother God. So I didn't explain.

"Have some tea," I said.

"No, I don't drink that stuff," Jaycia whispered. "You should never drink that stuff. They put bad stuff in the tea."

"The tea is good for you," I said. "The tea is from Mother God."

"God!" Jaycia almost yelled it.

My eyes got wide. When you said the word like that it was a bad word. Not an Abomination, but the very biggest Mistake.

"I swear, Zylynn, as soon as I start to hope you're the one who has a brain it seems like you're as stupid as everyone else here," Jaycia said.

It felt like she had pinged my heart.

"You're supposed to drink the tea," I said.

Somehow the rest of us were still asleep. None of our heads were popping up. None of us rustling or crying.

"I won't. I can't," she said. Her eyes were super wet, almost like she was having a nightmare, but she was awake. "You don't get it. I was hoping you would, but no one gets it. No one here gets anything."

"Gets what?" I asked.

Jaycia shook her head and kicked off her sheet. Suddenly the butt of her white shorts was in my face. "Get down," she said. "Get off. I'm finding food."

"You can't," I said. "You can't get out of bed. It's a Mistake."

But I was already moving down the ropes because she would step on my hands if I didn't.

On the sandy floor, she stared at me. "If I don't get food, I'll keep having nightmares. You coming?"

I didn't like this. I didn't know what to do. I had to keep everyone in bed. I had to stop the nightmares. Which one should I do when I couldn't do both at once?

She didn't wait for me to answer. She moved through the room, the sand on the floor sticking in bits to her bare feet. She pushed aside the metal door and then she was out.

I ran after her.

At the door, I took a big breath, a huge one. Then I plowed through it.

It wasn't dark out there. Spotlights hung from every building spilling light onto every path. But it was so bright in the dorms, it took my eyes a minute to adjust. Then I saw her, legs and arms flailing as she sprinted toward the Dining Hall.

I took off after her, following her through the double doors into the large room.

The tables were empty, of course. It was the middle of the night. But Jaycia did not stop, she didn't pause, she didn't wonder at how strange it was to be in this room all by ourselves. She kept running until she was through the archway at the back of the room.

I gasped. We weren't allowed in there, in the kitchen.

I tiptoed past the empty tables, ignoring the sounds of my own stomach, ignoring the panic of my own heart, ignoring, ignoring, ignoring.

I tilted my head through the arch and peeked in.

She stood still, legs splayed, arms wide to each side holding open black refrigerator doors, She turned to look at me. And, finally, she laughed.

"Zylynn," she said. "Look!"

"No," I said. "This is an Abomination. Mother God could strike you dead."

"There's so much food!" Jaycia laughed again. She turned. In her hand she held the largest, yellowest block of cheese I'd ever seen.

My stomach tried to climb up my throat, to escape my body in order to get that cheese.

"Want some?" she said.

I took a step toward her. She nodded. She held the cheese out even farther.

It wasn't my legs walking, it was my stomach, pushing me forward and then I wasn't stepping, I was sliding, skipping, running across the kitchen until my teeth had sunk into the cheese right where it rested in her palm.

Abomination.

We ate the whole block, passing it back and forth, taking bites right on top of each other's teeth marks. When it was gone, our stomachs twisted in a new kind of pain.

Abomination.

A few days later, she was gone. A few weeks later, so was I.

I walk into the kitchen but I'm still alone and I don't like that. I walk down the stairs and into the family room that's connected to the screen porch that's connected to the yard that holds the swing set. Charita is in the room, but she's so quiet I almost miss her. She's sitting alone at the very back of the room, staring at a small screen. It paints a bright line across the profile of her face.

More lights in Darkness. So many lights in Darkness. They didn't tell us this at all in Outside Studies.

She doesn't see me. I wonder if she can't see me while she's looking at the glowing book.

I take a small step closer to her. I don't want to scare her the way Louis scares me when he starts walking into the Pink Stripes Room. Even though I won't touch her. Even though I kind of want to feel her dark hair and her arms the way they held me in the car yesterday. I take another smaller step.

She turns and gasps. "Zylynn!" she says. "You scared me."

I retreat immediately. *I wasn't going to touch you. I promise. And even if I was, I wouldn't hurt you.*

"No, no, no," she says like I'm one of the guard dogs at the gate who were always getting yelled at for eating stuff they shouldn't. "I'm sorry. I don't mean you scared me. I didn't see you is all. You startled me."

Startle (v.): to disturb or agitate suddenly by surprise or alarm

Even when I know the words it's not helping me understand.

I'm walking backward, back toward the steps.

"It's OK, Zylynn," she says. "You're welcome anywhere in this house."

I freeze.

I am?

"Is there something you want to do today?"

My eyes bug so far out of their sockets I'm sure they'll roll onto the floor. I can't believe she asked me that. There are those words again: *What do you want*?

The answer is so simple. It was so simple the whole time. She asks me what I want, I pick it out, I get it. That's how it worked in Target with the Shoppers. Could it be that easy?

I open my mouth to tell her, to say it, to end this.

I want to go home.

Instead my voice says, so quietly even my own ears can hardly hear it, "What is that?"

My jaw drops. Curiosity somehow snuck into my lungs and out of my throat. I can't make myself stop wanting to know about a book that glows.

"This?" Charita laughs. She points to the thing on the desk in front of her.

I nod.

That was my first curious question in Darkness. My heart burns with shame. I shouldn't want to know about the glowing book. I shouldn't be sorry for scaring Charita. I shouldn't be wishing that I lived with a woman all the time the way that Elsie and Junior and Jakey get to. A woman who hugs you when you're feeling sad and who feeds you when you're feeling hungry. I shouldn't be here, right now, at all. I should be upstairs praying. I should be trying to escape. I should be asking this woman to take me home and leave me there and never see me again.

Curiosity. It's terrifying.

"It's a tablet. Like a laptop," Charita says. "A computer."

I tilt my head. We had computers on the compound but they were always bigger than my head and shoulders combined. This glowing book is barely the size of Charita's hand.

"Come here," she says. "I'll show you."

Charita asked me what I want to do. I didn't say go home. I ignore that wobbly-ness.

I walk over to her.

On the screen there are dancing turtles, each with a different number painted on the front of their shells.

"It's a math game," Charita says. "See?"

She guides my hand as we click on numbers that are listed on the sides. We just have to choose the number that solves the equations on the turtles' shells.

"Think you got it?" Charita asks. She backs up, watching me at the glowing book from a few feet away.

And, then, I really am playing all by myself.

Their voices are in my room again that night. Charita's voice. Louis's is just little grumbles.

"She knows her math," Charita is saying. "So there's that."

Louis grumbles.

"We'll have to take her to the school in a few weeks. Get her tested. See what grade to put her into in the fall."

Louis grumbles.

Her is me. That's all I know. It makes nerves jump around in the veins on my wrists like lightning bolts inside me.

I won't be here in the fall. I won't be here in a few weeks. I won't. *Right, Father?*

But I feel my face flush. I wouldn't be here right now, maybe, if I had asked to go home instead of playing on the computer today.

Louis is still grumbling.

"Is something wrong, babe?" Charita says.

Babe is Louis, or sometimes Charita. They call each other that. And other things like *love* and *mine*. It's too confusing for me. It's too hard to remember that all of those things mean Louis. Especially since *babe* sounds like a baby and Louis is almost a hundred years old and *love* is a thing, not a person and *mine* is a bad word and *dad* I've never heard of before.

"She hates me," Louis says.

I wonder if they put their voices in my room on purpose or if they don't know how it happens or if they even know that it's happening. I don't think so. I think I'm being sneaky. Or maybe it's Father Prophet putting their voices in here to give me some hints about how to get out of here, out of Darkness, back Inside.

"She's scared is all," Charita says.

Louis grumbles. Then his voice comes clear. "My own daughter hates me."

Daughter. There's that word again. One of the other words for me.

"She hates me." He won't stop saying it.

My heart feels heavy then, sinking in my body toward the

mattress springs. His voice is so soft and sad and that word *daughter*, the way he says it, is so nice and light, I almost don't want to hate him.

I have to hate him.

"She's terrified," Charita says.

He sighs. "I know. I'm glad you've gotten somewhere. But . . . now . . . I finally have her back and . . ."

I can't hear anything else.

He thinks he has me. He thinks I belong here. I have to get away from him.

Father, how do I do it?

I have five days to figure it out.

Eleven

LOUIS IS THERE IN THE MORNING again when I'm up and at the window trying to remember the exact gray of Father's eyes. I'm dressed in the pink pajamas. But he's not dressed the same way as usual: black pants, white shirt, tie. Instead it's shorts and an orange T-shirt that hangs almost to his knees. His eyes are red and there are black half-moons beneath them.

He stares at me from the doorway for a minute and I stare back. There are lots of voices beneath us. Different from the normal someone/someones who come and make Elsie or Junior disappear for parts of the day. Instead their feet are banging against the floors downstairs, going back and forth. There's a lot of laughing.

If Louis wasn't standing in my door I might try it again, myself. Laughing. I might see if it could possibly feel as good coming out of my mouth as it sounds going into my ears.

"Morning, Zylynn," he says in that soft way. And even though that's how his voice sounds I'm still afraid of him. He's an Outsider, an Agent of Darkness, a Liar so skilled I haven't been able to pick up on a single one of his lies. "We have to go somewhere today," he says. "Just you and me, OK?"

This is it. Finally, I think. *Home.*

I'm relieved I didn't have to ask. I've never asked for anything before.

Home. Inside. It feels weird, heavy in my heart. I clutch my turtle in my hand.

Why can't I bring the things I like about Darkness with me Inside? Why can't I bring laughing and toys and food and Elsie's smiles and Charita's hugs and leave the terrifying nights and the headaches and the confusion and Louis behind? The Light is supposed to be made of everything good. Mother God is supposed to be the source of all good things. So Turtle must come from Mother God. So why can't he come back with me?

"There are some people downstairs who want to meet you first. If you're afraid . . . that's OK . . . maybe you can manage a small wave?"

He pauses but I'm not hearing him. I'm thinking about going back Inside. I'm thinking about Father Prophet and my heart is hammering all the way down in my belly because I can't remember the exact shade of his eyes or the contours of his cheeks. I can't remember what he sounded like when his voice wasn't booming off the stone benches in Chapel. I can't remember his smile.

I'm going to get the worst punishment there is. He won't

let me eat until my stomach deflates back in between my ribs. I'll be pinged at the fence all day every day for the next three days.

My blood is rushing close to panic. I should be happy.

I'm happy to go home, I tell myself.

I'm happy for what will happen after-after. Once the punishment is over and I go back to waking up with everyone else, hot sand on my feet, cold morning showers, oatmeal. I'm happy for when that becomes normal and something I understand. I'm happy for when I forget the Darkness ever happened to me.

But with each day I've spent out here it feels like it will take one more day to forget Darkness and that's one more day that Father Prophet will punish me. At this point I'll be punished right up to my Ceremony.

I choke in air.

Louis is talking. He says we're going out, the two of us. He's taking me home. I should smile at him.

"So get dressed, OK?" he says, and he steps out and closes the door. I fly through the Pink Stripes Room looking for the white shorts, white T-shirt, white underwear I showed up in. I check the drawers and the closet where all of my newly colorful clothes call out their lies to me.

Not mine. They can't be my clothes. Nothing can be mine because I belong to someone else.

See, Father, I remember. But I'm confused. The Darkness has twisted me.

The old white clothes are gone. The new white clothes aren't here either. Charita must have taken them and hidden them somewhere. He is a Liar and she is a crook and they're both evil and maybe I am too, now.

In a final attempt to find them, I dive under the bed and come face-to-face with the two round white plates piled carefully with all of the food I've been saving. Except it's different. I'm so surprised, I bump my head on the bottom of the mattress.

"You OK in there?" Louis calls.

I didn't realize he was standing in the hallway waiting for me. I only have a few seconds to figure out what to do.

The food is still there, in front of me. Charita didn't steal any of it. Or Louis. Or anyone. Each strawberry, each pancake, each crust of peanut butter sandwich is still there, under the bed. But it's different. I've never seen this before, but I know what it is.

> **Tupperware** (n.): a range of plastic containers used for storing food

The strawberries are packed into a big, deep one. The bits of peanut butter sandwich are stuffed into one that's long and flat. The chips and cookies and pretzels are all divided and stacked in separate plastic bags. Who did this?

I don't have time to figure it out.

Instead I grab the backpack that Elsie left in here when she was playing School last night and I stuff it. The strawberries go in first. Then all the things that have meat. The peanut butter crusts next. The cookies last. I don't know how I'll sneak it into the Girls' Dorm. But I'll hide it under my blankets once I get there. It worked when I hid the orange and the banana so it will work with this food too. I don't know why I didn't think to do this when I was there before.

Louis knocks on the door. "You almost ready?"

I bump my head again. I pull on the first pair of shorts and T-shirt in the top drawer. No time to search for my whites anymore.

I take a step toward the door and spin around. I find the last thing I'm looking for. He's on my gold carpet, lying on his green shell so that his yellow underside is all exposed. I dive for Turtle and stuff him in my pocket.

If Mother God is the source of all things good, she'll be proud of me for bringing good things into the Light.

I'm still rushing so I swing the door open so fast it bounces against the wooden wall. Louis jumps like he was standing too close to it.

"You all ready?" he asks me.

I stare.

"You're going to take Elsie's backpack?"

I didn't even think about that. About how the backpack is Elsie's and Louis might not want me to take it. About how things belong to certain people here and sometimes that certain person isn't me.

"It's OK," he says. "Elsie can share."

I don't quite understand that word still. But I nod. He's taking me home now, so I smile. Louis smiles so huge I think his face may crack in half. His face is furry again, gray. Is that gray the color of Father's eyes? Why can't I remember?

"Well, I'd love to hear your voice but a smile is better than nothing," he says.

I wish he didn't look so kind.

I follow him down the stairs and at the bottom he freezes. I'm still behind him.

Standing in front of him are two people I've never seen before: a tall man standing so close to a short woman, his elbow is pressed against her shoulder. Their hair is full of every shade of gray and all I can do is look at it, search it strand by strand to see if I can come up with the right shade for Father's eyes. If I can do that, if I can remember that one thing, maybe I won't be punished. Even their faces, which are full of bumps and wrinkles, look a little gray. Is Father Prophet putting all of this gray in front of me to prove how awful I am for forgetting his eyes?

"Zylynn," Louis says, "you don't have to say anything but I promised your grandparents that they'd have a chance to meet you if they came over. Maybe you could give them a smile or a wave."

It's not only me staring at them. They're also staring at me.

I take another step so that I'm completely behind Louis, as if he's safe. He seems safe, now, but I know that's a lie.

Grandparent (n.): a parent of a parent

How did I not realize back at home that I didn't understand any of this vocabulary? How did I not know that in order to understand *grandparent* I'd have to first understand *parent*?

My brain flips and flips for it, but it was never on any of our lists.

Who are these people? Why do they care if I smile or wave at them? And Louis didn't just call them *grandparents*, he called them *your*. Mine. What does that mean? What could make another human mine?

My breath gets shaky behind his back and Louis sighs. "She's not ready," he says. "I'm sorry. It's . . . slow-going . . ."

The two gray heads nod. "She's here," the woman says. "She's safe. That's what matters."

I'm not safe. Yet.

"Whatever you need, son," the man says.

Then they're gone, down the stairs where Elsie and Junior and Jakey are still yelping and laughing. The Darkness must have twisted my brain so badly in under a week because I could swear their laughter sounds like tiny lightbulbs. Elsie's laugh is the loudest.

Elsie!

Will Louis let me take her? If I save someone, maybe my punishment won't be so bad. And maybe I'll have those little lightbulbs of laughing back Inside. It's another good thing I can bring to Mother God.

Louis turns around and looks down at me. His eyes are sharp in their veiny red cages.

We're alone in the room and he's scary again. I back up a few steps.

"You ready?" he says. It's like he's trying to make his voice as bouncy as possible. Like he's trying to sound like Elsie does downstairs, but he can't.

"I . . ." *Ask him. Just ask him.*

With Elsie there Father will be so pleased with me. I'll get my ceremony for sure. I'll get praised in Chapel for finding a new soul.

I'll finally be forgiven for eating that cheese.

"Yes, Zylynn?" Louis says.

It's hard to make my mouth say the words. "I . . . Can . . . Can Elsie . . . come . . . too?"

Relief floods my body cool and sure. I'm doing the right thing. *I'm doing it all for you.*

But Louis laughs. "Oh, Elsie doesn't need to come. She went to the doctor when she turned five."

"Huh?" I say before I can trap the sound.

"We're going to go meet your uncle Alan."

No.

"It's a short drive. We can do something fun afterward. But we have to meet your uncle. We can't put that off any longer."

No.

"It's a Saturday, so he's coming in special just for you. There won't be anyone else there. Just you, me, your uncle."

No.

"We've got to get you healthy. That's priority number one."

Louis takes a step toward the door. I take another up the stairs.

I thought I was going home. Again.

"Zylynn?" he says. "We've got to go."

I'm not going to let it be like before when I thought Charita was taking me back Inside. I have to ask. I put the word together in my stomach. The letters form there, they arrange into the right order in my ribs, and I push them through my mouth until the sound comes out, raspy and hoarse. I speak to the kidnapper. "Where?"

Louis smiles again and his eyes get a little wet at the same time. "Alan's office," he says. "The doctor's office."

No.

I cannot get in a car with him, just me and him, and go somewhere else, another compound, another place, another stranger.

I have to ask him. I have to be brave. "I . . . I wanted . . ."

Louis's smile gets bigger. "Yes?" he says. Like he wants to know what I'm going to say. Like he'll give me everything I want.

"I wanted to go . . . somewhere . . ." I can't make my mouth say the word *home.* I'm too terrified.

Once I ask, he'll either say yes or no. If he says yes, everything is great. But what will I do if he says no?

"I wanted to . . . go . . ."

When I've stopped talking for a long time, Louis sighs.

"We have to do this, kiddo. We have to go to the doctor, even if you're scared. I promise it will be OK. But it's not a choice," he says. "We need to get you healthy."

I shake my head, a tiny *no.* I'm not sure if he sees it.

"We can do whatever you want to do after we see your uncle Alan, OK?" he says.

So that's it. Another strange place. Another strange Liar looking at me. Touching me. Then I can ask to go home.

I swallow the scream, force it back down my throat and all the way into my heels. I can't let myself get too twisted.

I take another step backward, up, toward the pink stripes and the window that feels safe even though they aren't.

Louis sighs.

"What if Charita comes along?" he asks, the corners of his lips pointing toward the wood floor. "Would that be better?"

A tiny jerk of my head. My heart starts beating again. The scream dissolves silently into the steps beneath me.

It will be better with Charita.

But it shouldn't be.

I don't have to flip in my brain for the word *doctor.* There was one on the compound, but I forgot all about him until I heard Louis say the word. We all went to see him once a year, the day before our birthday.

In the backseat of their car, I study my flip-flops and wonder if this doctor will be the same.

* * *

"Zylynn?" he said when I walked into the white room from the white hallway where I was waiting with the ten or fifty Children Inside the Light who share a birthday.

We were in the back of the compound, past the Girls' and Boys' Dorms, past the Teen Girls' and Teen Boys' and Men's Dorms, past the Dining Hall and the Chapel and the Exercise Fields. We were in the third circle where we almost never went. We were as back as we could go, a thirty- or forty-minute walk from the front gate. Only one building was behind this one. It was the big white-and-silver one with rooms built right on top of other rooms; the building that we weren't ever allowed to enter because it was where Father Prophet lived. Just being that close to it made me feel icky and guilty. Even though this was before I ever did anything bad. This was before Jaycia did anything worse than laugh in the night.

Bortank, one of the teen-boy Messengers, had come with a note that removed me from Exercise for the day. That never happened unless you had committed an Abomination. And I was pretty sure I hadn't. And I was pretty sure Mother God wouldn't let me be punished unjustly. But I was still nervous.

"Zylynn?" the doctor said again. I recognized this man, but I didn't know he was the doctor. I couldn't remember my last birthday, which was the last time I would have seen the doctor.

I nodded.

"I'm Brother Tomlinkin."

I nodded again. I'd seen him in Chapel. I knew the names of everyone Inside except the newest of new souls.

"Do you remember coming to see me last year?" he asked.

I shook my head and shifted on my feet.

It wasn't Brother Tomlinkin who was making me uncomfortable. He wasn't an Outsider or a Liar or any other terrible thing. It was being in such an empty room. It was being so far from the rest of us. I hadn't ever been with just one person in a room before, that I could remember. And before I crossed the door, Brother Tomlinkin had been the only, only person in the room. It made me feel queasy.

"OK, well, I'm a doctor," he said. "I was trained Outside, a long time ago, so it's all official and everything."

That sentence made me gulp.

"Father Prophet wants to make sure all of the Children Inside the Light are healthy. So I check everybody out—boys, girls, men—once a year."

It was for Father Prophet.

I nodded. "OK," I said.

Brother Tomlinkin motioned to the little paper-covered bed that was behind him. "Hop on up," he said.

He explained that he was going to take my blood. He told me to be brave while he stuck a needle in my arm and I held my breath and tried not to feel it. It wasn't really my arm anyway, I told myself. Not really my blood. I belong to someone else.

When the blood snaked out, through the tube and into a vial, I expected it to be white or Light, like us. But it was dark, almost the color of the clay paths all around the compound. I watched it ooze into the tube and I wondered how a color that rich could be hidden inside our pale bodies.

Everything else with Brother Tomlinkin was easy. I stood on a scale and put my back against a wall while he held something on the top of my head. I let him shine bright lights in my eyes. He knocked a hammer against my knee but it didn't hurt. He stuck things in my ears and nose and mouth and put headphones in his ears to listen to my chest. He didn't smile or speak in that soft feathery way like they do in Darkness, but he said my name a lot and gave clear instructions.

"How old are you turning tomorrow, Zylynn?" he asked at the end. He was frowning over a clipboard. "Eight?"

"Twelve," I said. I was pulling a shoe back on.

Brother Tomlinkin's frown deepened. "Twelve?" he said. It was a loud word. Louder than anyone dared to speak Inside. "Are you sure?"

I didn't jump. "Yes," I said.

He made me take my shoes back off and stand on the scale again. His frown got deeper and deeper and I got lonelier and lonelier in this room with only one human. My ears stretched and shook trying to hear the sounds of normal life: the ball hitting the fence in Exercise, Brother Frankater demanding we run faster, the whistles of the Caretakers telling us to line up for dinner. Instead I was alone in this room with this frowning man.

"How are you sleeping?" he asked.

I didn't understand the question. I tilted my head at him but he stared at the clipboard.

"How are you sleeping?" he said again.

"In my bed," I answered finally. "The bed, I mean."

He looked at me then, shaking his head. "No, no, no. I mean, how do you sleep at night? Do you sleep well?"

I sucked on my lower lip. Brother Tomlinkin was an authority figure with an office closer to Father Prophet's house than I had ever been. He was one of the most important men on the compound, one of Father's Officials. It was important to please and obey him. But I didn't understand.

"I didn't know it was like school," I said finally.

He scrunched his eyebrows like he was confused.

"I didn't know it was something I had to do well at."

He made a clicking-type noise with his mouth and shook his head.

"You're really twelve?"

"Yes," I said. I would be eight if he wanted me to be. Anything to get me out of there.

"You can go," he said.

And I did.

I didn't see Brother Tomlinkin too many times after that. Not at Chapel or the Dining Hall or anywhere on the clay paths. Sometime, days or months after, he was gone.

Uncle Alan's room looks a lot like Brother Tomlinkin's. But Uncle Alan does not look like Brother Tomlinkin.

Another man introduces himself as Pete, Alan's nurse, whatever that is. He leads us through a bright room with couches, down a short, bright hallway, and into a room with three chairs and a sink and a little paper-covered table against the back wall.

Everything is white and everywhere there are lights. Not on the walls. I don't think they know about lightbulbs on the walls in Darkness because I haven't seen one anywhere. But tubes of light run through the middle of every ceiling. And lamps rest on most of the counters and surfaces. A big silver lamp reaches from the floor all the way above my head where I sit on the table, so bright it buzzes. The buzzing works its way into my ear canals, comfortable, familiar, relaxing.

I can see Uncle Alan through the open door, not coming in yet. Not looking at me yet. Instead he's holding a folder shut between two splayed hands, looking at it and taking deep breaths.

I can't stop staring at his beard.

His head is completely bald, so the lights reflect off it. His eyes are pale blue like the sky in the middle of the day when the sun is blocking out most of its color. His skin is pale, almost like he could belong Inside. And his beard—which curls across his face from ear to ear, over his chin and above his upper lip—is yellow. It's a shade of yellow I haven't seen before except for one place: my own head.

It makes me want to hop off this table and pull a chair over in front of him, and stand on it, and take a bit of my hair between my fingers and pull it away from my head and hold it up against his chin to see how close the color really is.

I watch the beard open and close as Uncle Alan takes a big

breath and comes into the gloriously bright Doctor Room.

"Zylynn," he says. That's all. He's staring at me. I'm staring at his beard.

The room is so still I start to get itchy. Finally I say "yes" because I just have to get through this one thing, then I can ask to go home.

"I haven't seen you since you were—" He holds his hands only about a foot apart. "I haven't seen you since my sister . . . since Tessie—"

"I know." Louis's voice is suddenly loud and between us.

Uncle Alan turns to Louis where he sits in one of the chairs next to the bed and the words run over and over in my head. *I haven't seen you since Tessie . . . I haven't seen you since Tessie . . .*

Tessie . . . Tessie . . . Tessie . . .

Was he talking to me? It sounded like it. Was Uncle Alan saying he's seen me before somehow?

Tessie . . . Tessie . . . Tessie . . .

Why does that sound so familiar?

"I didn't think I'd ever get to . . ." Uncle Alan is looking at Louis now, his words coming choppy and staticky out of his mouth.

"I know, I know," Louis says again.

Then, suddenly, everyone is crying. Louis is crying and clutching Uncle Alan, their backs jerking as they take loud breaths in between sobs, Charita is mumbling into a tissue in her chair while black tears run over her cheeks, and I've never seen so many people cry and I've never seen any man who is so big cry and I've never been in a room like this and

Tessie . . . Tessie . . . Tessie . . .

And, and, and I'm not afraid of Uncle Alan. I'm really not. His beard is my color. His eyes are so kind. His office is so bright. But I'm afraid that I'm not afraid because he's on the Outside in Darkness where there are Liars and everything gets twisted in my brain and twisted in my brain and twisted in my brain until

Tessie . . . Tessie . . . Tessie . . .

Until, then, something leaks over my cheeks and I'm crying too and I know I've cried before but I think I must have been very small because I don't remember it feeling like this, this wet on my cheeks, this gooey in my nose, this loud in my chest, this exhausting in my brain so

Tessie . . . Tessie . . . Tessie . . .

Charita stands to hand me the box of tissues and when I put my hand out for one I think she thinks I'm reaching for her or maybe I am reaching for her because then she's on the table next to me and my head is on her shoulder and her arm is squeezing me and it's like she doesn't care that tears and snot are spilling all over her T-shirt and Louis and Uncle Alan are still holding each other and I don't know why I'm crying but maybe

Tessie . . . Tessie . . . Tessie . . .

I'm crying because I want to know why I'm crying and I want to know what crying hard feels like and if the Darkness can make me cry then maybe it can also make me laugh and if it can I want to know that and I want to know more about these people like why Louis's eyes look like mine and why Uncle Alan has my hair on his chin and why I like Charita best even though she has nothing of mine and

Tessie . . . Tessie . . . Tessie . . .

It's scary because I'm not supposed to want to know anything about anything.

Curiosity is leaking out my eyes.

It feels like we stop crying all at once and everyone takes a huge breath. The three of them sputter into a short burst of laughter and I wonder how they do it and if laughing could be so close to crying.

When Charita gets up, I lie back on the table, even though no one told me to. I take another deep breath.

I never knew crying would feel this good. Or having cried. I can't believe it. How relaxed my shoulders are. How loose my joints are. My arms and legs feel like jelly. My heart is slow and steady.

So when Louis sits down next to Charita, and Uncle Alan opens the folder and smiles at me, I feel that pinch in my cheek again.

"How old are you now, Zylynn?"

"Twelve," I say. "Thirteen in four days."

My voice sounds more like my own than it has in a long, long time. Or, maybe, ever.

Uncle Alan does the same things as Brother Tomlinkin with the blood and the headphones and the hammer that doesn't hurt. He asks a lot of questions and I answer them all. And not because Louis and Charita said I have to. Only because I'm so relaxed I'm not thinking.

When I'm done, they ask me to go sit back in the waiting room. I hop off the table and leave the little room with the bright lamps. The door closes behind me.

Then I realize I don't know what a waiting room is.

I freeze with the door to my back and then I hear Uncle Alan heave a huge sigh. "Well," I hear him say. "I don't know why I think this but something in my gut tells me she's going to be OK. She's a tough cookie."

Charita is crying again. "Those bruises!" she says. "All over her."

"Yeah," Uncle Alan says. "But they'll heal. They already are. She's malnourished. There might be some more news when we get the blood work back from the lab. She's probably anemic from the lack of good food, which means she bruises easily . . . I'm not saying those bruises are the normal wear and tear of childhood . . . they're . . . awful . . . just . . . I was dreading worse."

They're talking about me. This is kind of like when the words sneak into the Pink Stripes Room but also kind of not like that because I could walk away this time but my feet don't move.

"Healthy food, lots of food, a multivitamin, a calcium supplement, and a steady routine will go a long way," Uncle Alan says. "I found a specialist for you guys. Here, take her card.

Therapy will be a priority, a big one, probably for the rest of her life."

> **Therapy** (n.): the treatment of disease or disorders, as by some remedial, rehabilitating, or curative process

Another one I didn't know that I didn't really know.

"Of course," Charita says.

"But she, this therapist, says not yet. Let her get used to things at home first. Spend as much time as a family as possible. You should call the therapist soon, though. She'll have some tips for you two."

"Thanks," Louis says.

"Really, nourishment will do a whole lot of good for her now," Uncle Alan says. "We start there. It's going to take time, but it's going to be OK."

"It's going to be OK," Louis says, his voice barely a whisper.

Then there's a hand on the doorknob and I scurry down the hall. I don't think they catch me.

When we're back in the car—Louis behind the steering wheel, Charita next to him, me in the seat behind her—I see her squeeze his hand and nod.

"So, Zylynn, do you want to tell me where it is you'd like to go now?"

I stare at him in the little mirror over his head and my heart hammers in my chest: *Home, home, home . . .*

But I'm still thinking *Tessie . . . Tessie . . . Tessie . . .*

Why is that word sticking to me like too-long hair after a sweaty Exercise?

Louis is still talking. "Grandma and Grandpa will be happy to stay at our house all day, so we can keep this little outing going," he says.

Home. Take me home. That's what I'm supposed to say. That's what Father would want me to say.

Something is sad about thinking that, even though it's what I want.

It is. I promise.

"I . . . Will you . . . Can we . . . Can I . . ."

I'm going to say it. I know I'm going to say it.

But then Charita interrupts me and says, "Or maybe we should go to lunch first? After we eat, you can tell us what you were thinking of."

I know I should ask them to take me back to the compound right now. I don't deserve another meal. My stomach folds in on itself. If I say "home" I won't eat for a long, long time. I skipped breakfast for Uncle Alan.

"Lunch," I choose. *Lunch, then home.*

I bite my bottom lip so hard it bleeds. *Is this enough punishment, Father?*

Twelve

THE ROAD VIBRATES AGAINST THE TIRES: *Tessie . . . Tessie . . . Tessie . . .*

The wind rattles the window: *Tessie . . . Tessie . . . Tessie . . .*

My brain whispers to my ears: *Tessie . . . Tessie . . . Tessie . . .*

We are quiet in the car.

Thirteen

GOING OUT TO LUNCH MEANS EATING somewhere that's not Louis's and Charita's and Elsie's and Junior's and Jakey's kitchen and it means that Charita and Louis sit instead of stand at counters and shout about food over their shoulders. The three of us sit at a round wooden table in a room full of Outsiders sitting at other tables. The sun is streaming in through the window and the smell of food is everywhere and the flowers in the middle of the table are the most colors I've ever seen all pushed together, so I decide not to be afraid.

After lunch I will ask them to take me home. I'll go back Inside with a full stomach so my punishment will not hurt as badly.

A lady wrapped in pockets comes to our table with a notebook in her palm.

Something white and squishy is crushed between her teeth. She snaps it in her mouth. "Can I get you folks started with some drinks?"

I look at her. Her hair is light and wispy with a reddish-pinkish hue. It's not like mine. It's not like Uncle Alan's.

Louis speaks at her and she writes something down.

"Zylynn," Charita says. "What would you like to drink, honey?"

My eyes go wide. No, not honey. Honey is delicious but it's sticky and gooey and it's not good unless you also have water to drink. It's kind of liquid-y, but it's not meant for drinking.

If she wants to give me honey, OK, but I can't drink it. I take a deep breath and say it: "No, not to drink."

No. Have I ever said that word in my life?

Charita looks confused. So do Louis and the woman wrapped in pockets.

"What?" the woman says.

I've lost track of how many words I've left out here now. I've given up.

"I can't drink honey," I say. "It's too gooey."

Charita and Louis laugh and the woman wrapped in pockets turns a little pink. "I wasn't offering you honey," Charita says. "It's a nickname. I was calling you 'honey.' It's a term of affection."

> **Nickname** (n.): a name added to or substituted for the proper name of a person, place, etc., as in affection, ridicule, or familiarity

Affection (n.): fond attachment or devotion, positive feeling or emotion

I nod. I sort of understand.

"So, honey," Charita says, smiling at me and I realize I'm smiling back. "What would you like to drink?"

I nod. I can do this. "Milk," I say. It's better than water.

The pocket lady snaps that white stuff again. She doesn't look at me. "Whole, half, skim, one percent or two percent?" she says.

At the same time Louis says, "Are you sure you don't want to try soda?"

"Louis!" Charita says, almost like she's angry but she's still smiling.

"What?" Louis says. "You heard Alan; she can use all the calories she can get."

"All the cal*cium* she can get too," Charita says.

Louis shrugs. He's smiling. She's smiling. "We're celebrating," he says.

I'm still smiling even though I don't know what they're talking about, what we're celebrating. Then I'm smiling because I realize that I'm smiling.

I'm not smiling. I'm lying to them, I promise.

"Soda," I say. I don't know what it is, but it's easier than figuring out that other question the Pocket Lady was asking in percentages.

"Coke, Diet Coke, Sprite, ginger ale, Dr Pepper, orange,

grape, or root beer?" The woman is still tapping her pen against her notebook, waiting for me to answer.

Why does Outside have so many choices? And how can all of these choices be so terrible? How can the Outside be full of lies when I'm making the decisions? Is the Darkness making me lie to myself?

Is that what happened to Jaycia? Did she choose things and lie to herself until she forgot us? And now she's stuck here. But she's thirteen now. So she doesn't have the choices and the food anymore. The Darkness addicted her and now she's stuck, doomed and tortured.

I look at Charita until she answers "root beer" for me.

It's in front of me quickly, brown and bubbling and tasting like liquefied sugar, delicious.

Charita nudges Louis and hands me a piece of plastic with words on it. "Honey," she says. We all smile. "This is what they serve for lunch. These are your options. Can you read it and decide what you'd like?"

She's speaking, slowly, carefully, like it's really important what I choose.

I look at the plastic she's put in front of me. I know what it is, but I've never seen one before.

Menu (n.): a list of the dishes served at a meal; bill of fare

I stare and stare and my brain sways in my head. It's like an Outside Studies Vocabulary List for my taste buds. Spaghetti, hamburger, club sandwich, BLT, French fries, onion rings, chicken salad, macaroni salad, potato salad. How can there be so many kinds of salad?

I read the whole thing, once, twice, three times and I must be looking at it for a long time because when I take a break to sip my root beer, Louis and Charita are staring at me.

"Can you decide for me?" I ask quietly.

Charita sucks air quickly up her nose. Louis shakes his head, his face getting red.

Charita reaches across the table for my hand. I let her rest hers on top of mine.

Touching: that's different about the Outside too. And I like it. Evil, Liar, dirty? Or does it matter if I'm also lying to myself?

I cannot be thinking this way. I have to go home. After lunch.

"Zylynn," Charita says, slowly again. "Is it too hard to read?"

They think I'm stupid.

"I know how to read," I burst. The words are hot and loud in my mouth. I didn't know I could make words that loud. "I know what hamburger is and what spaghetti is and what chicken salad is," I say. Even though I don't. Whoever heard of salad made from a chicken? "I want a hamburger," I say. Because I do. I want everything.

I yank my hand from under Charita's and brace myself against the back of the seat. I'm sure she'll slap me now. Or Louis will. Or they'll take away my lunch. Or something. There will be a punishment for being so loud.

Instead, Louis and Charita share another smile. "You can have whatever you want," he says.

When the Pocket Lady comes back I tell her I'll have the hamburger and the spaghetti. She looks confused but Louis says, "Give them to her. Both." His words don't sound soft when he talks to her.

She shrugs and disappears. The clicking of her shoes against the wood floor, the slurping through the straw as Charita and Louis take a sip, the hushed words of the strangers at tables nearby, they all say *Tessie . . . Tessie . . . Tessie . . .* in my ears.

I haven't seen you since Tessie . . .

"So, Uncle Alan had a lot to say in there today," Charita says. "Does anybody have any questions?"

She's being nice. I'm getting used to it that she's usually being nice. But I know *anybody* really means me.

Louis nods. "And you've been here for almost a week now. It must be pretty overwhelming. Any questions for us, Zylynn?"

Who is Tessie?

That's what Curiosity wants to ask. She's crawling onto my tongue, trying to make me form the syllables, ask the question. And I think Louis and Charita can give her the answer. They know who Tessie is. I think they'd tell me. And I think it might be the truth. And I think I'd know if they were lying. Because I think there might be something I'm starting to remember.

My mouth is open, ready to ask, but all of my sounds stay deep inside me, terrified. Because I think it's something I used to know. And once I know I'm afraid I'll never not-know again.

When can I go home?

That's what I should ask. But there's still my hamburger and spaghetti. There's still the taste of BLT and chicken tenders and French fries to learn. There's still the feeling of laughter in my throat, of making someone else smile, of crying so hard until I'm relaxed again. There's still a million more games on the tablet and all of the colors that I haven't seen against my skin.

I can feel these things changing me, mixing me up until I'm a different Zylynn. Or until I am *Zylynn,* my own separate thing with edges and fingers, with a voice and a brain, instead of a blurry part of the Light.

I need to ask to go home before I break off even more, spinning into the Darkness like a star falling from the sky.

I need to get home before three and a half more days go by. I need to be there for my Thirteenth Ceremony. I need to be there so that I can keep going to school and start to train for the Work the day after, to win new souls. I need to be there so that I can move into the Teen Girls' Dorm in the second circle. I need to be there at my Thirteenth Ceremony so that I can still be there when I turn twenty and I'm able to go back into the Darkness, armed with the ability to beat it.

I need to get Inside before I'm stuck in Darkness for good.

Itheera stood in the back of the Chapel, a slip of a silhouette in the doorways with the setting sun shining bright behind her.

We strained to see her from the front stone benches where the girls sat, but we couldn't crane our necks around enough. We fidgeted with our fingers and the hems of our white shorts and T-shirts. It was dark in the Chapel. Not pitch-black, but the lights were out and the sinking sun in the high windows made the air gray and foggy. The dark was OK, because Father Prophet said it was, but it still made us nervous.

We waited patiently until Itheera started to sing.

"Oh Mother God
Oh Light of all Lights
Oh Protectress and Fortress and Enchantress of Light
I am yours."

Her voice floated down the aisle in the middle of the stone Chapel until it reached Father Prophet where he sat in his throne on the altar, his cape spilling behind him onto the floor. We glued our tongues to the roofs of our mouths, keeping our voices inside. We all knew the song, we all sang it together every day. But this was the one day in the world that was Itheera's day and not everyone's and we were supposed to stay silent.

"Oh Mother God
I am Light
I am yours."

When her voice faded away, Itheera stepped down the aisle and we gasped. She looked so different. She had traded in the girls' white shorts for the long, white skirt with layers and layers of lace that the women and the teen girls wore on the formalist occasions. Her white T-shirt was now a silk blouse. Her lips and cheeks were pinker than we'd ever seen them, her eyes were bluer. Her light brown hair was clipped back with a million sparkling silver pins because she would never cut it again.

Her bare feet stepped gingerly down the aisle. A smile jerked back and forth on her face. This was the only time we saw girls in these clothes until they became full-grown women. This was the only time we saw most girls smile.

And after today we would see Itheera less and less. She'd move out of the Girls' Dorm in the first circle and into the Teen Girls' Dorm in the second circle. She'd go to school with us in the mornings at first, then, over the years, she'd be there for fewer and fewer hours until her days were spent mostly training to gather new souls. She'd disappear slowly from the routine of our lives until, when she turned twenty, she'd finally be fully trained and able to withstand weeks or months in the Darkness. We would almost forget about her; she'd only show up at the Feasts.

We'd seen it happen again and again as girls we knew turned into women. We were waiting for it to be our turn.

At the end of the aisle, Father Prophet reached out his hands and took both of hers. He pulled her up the metal steps, onto the stage with him.

She stood in front of him, his hands on her shoulders.

And then we all sang. We echoed back the song to her in unison, not even owning our voices, being nothing but a force of Light in the dimming Chapel.

"Happy birthday, Itheera," Father said. "Are you ready to spread your Light?"

"I am, Father," she said, just like we practiced.

He sat down in his big chair behind her. "Go ahead, Itheera," he said.

She stood in the spot where it was almost every day only him. Then she whispered, "Judge me worthy."

We held our breath. This was the moment when Mother God would decide if Itheera was Light enough, if she had been obedient enough to Father, if she had resisted Curiosity enough to embrace Mother's Light fully.

Slowly Itheera raised her hands, her palms facing inward, her knuckles facing us, until her elbows were almost straight.

Then, with a huge, grand buzz, Mother God lit all of the lightbulbs in the Chapel on the walls and the ceiling and even the tiny ones lining the center aisle on the floor and we all whooped and applauded for Itheera as she finally let herself smile.

Father Prophet stood and put his large hands back on Itheera's silk shoulders.

"It is good you are here, Itheera. It is most pleasing to Mother God that you are here the minute you turn thirteen. You have pleased her. You will always have the Darkness in you, but if you listen to me, you will always be a Child Inside the Light."

He changed his tone to speak to all of us.

"Remember, my children, if you stray, you can always return Inside. But only until you turn thirteen."

We stood blinking in the blinding brightness, watching

Itheera smile, and waiting for our own turn.

That was the last Thirteenth Ceremony. It was long ago, weeks or months. Right before girls and boys started disappearing all the time.

I won't ask to go home yet, even though I should. Not until after the hamburger and the spaghetti.

I won't ask about Tessie, even though I want to.

I squint, looking in my brain for another question. In the six days I've been here, there's been so much I don't understand. Why they sleep in the dark. Why there is so much food. Where Louis goes when he says "work." Why Charita is there, right with the kids, all the time. Why they all choose to stay in that little green house the way we choose to stay Inside. There are so many things I don't know why they need: colors and computers and television and telephone and flip-flops and swing sets and toys and gray people in the house sometimes and pink stripes. I can't formulate any of these images and objects and wonderings into a full sentence. A question.

I see Pocket Lady coming back toward our table, her arms heavy with blue plates. (Whoever heard of a blue plate? Will it make my spaghetti taste differently than it should?)

I look at Charita and say: "When they call you Mom, is that like a nickname too?"

An easy question. She can answer with one word.

Instead she spins her glass of soda against her palm and

looks at Louis while he looks at her with those green eyes that are so like the ones in my head. Another wonder. Louis's eyes. Elsie's, Junior's, Jakey's eyes. Uncle Alan's hair. I can't make any of it into sentences.

"Well," Charita says, still talking all slowly like she has been all day. "No. Mom is more like a title than a nickname."

Pocket Lady starts clunking the plates onto the table and there's steam rising up from my red spaghetti that's so rich and sweet and thick in my nose I almost miss what Charita says next.

"They call me *Mom* because I'm their mother."

No. No you're not. The only Mother is God.

My head whips up to look at her. The steam is hot on my cheek. I don't want to be looking at her though, her brown eyes, her wavy hair, her pomegranate tea skin.

She keeps talking and I tear my eyes away, find a fork, and start digging it through the red-and-white pile on my plate.

"And they call Louis *Dad* because he's their father."

No. No. No.

My heart is hammering so huge and so hard I swear it's hitting my collarbone. She has to stop talking now. I can't hear these things. I can't even think about these things.

This is why they are Liars. This goes against the Ultimate Truth.

I put one noodle in my mouth and it burns my tongue so badly I spit it back onto the plate.

". . . and Louis is also your—"

My burned mouth says, shouts, "There is no Mother except God. There is no Father except the Prophet."

A few of the strangers turn to look at me. I said it louder than I've ever said anything in my life.

I don't care if I'm punished for saying it because it's the truth and Charita and Louis are lying. But Louis doesn't hit me. Charita doesn't slap me.

Instead, Louis's eyes leak on to his face again and he shakes his head back and forth over his sandwich.

Charita pats his hand. "We have to do this, babe," she says.

He moves his head the other way like he's nodding but he doesn't look up again.

Charita turns to me and she pulls my hand between the two of hers and I'm confused because her hands are warm and soft and nice and they shouldn't feel that way when I'm so angry at her.

"Zylynn," she says.

Then she freezes until I look at her.

"If you want believe in God, that's OK. If you want to think of God as your Mother, that's OK. If you want to think of God as the Mother of everything, that's OK, that might be right."

"It is right," I say, but my words are smaller, quieter now. She's calming me down against my will.

"But there are other mothers too, earthly mothers."

I shake my head.

Charita's hands loosen a little even though I don't want them to.

Louis takes a shaky breath. "Have you ever seen a pregnant woman, Zylynn?"

I raise my eyebrows at him and nod. They think I'm so stupid.

Louis has something in his hand now. The black rectangle he calls a phone. He holds it up to me and I can see an image on the screen. "Take it," he says.

Then it's in my palm, the one that isn't being squished and squeezed between Charita's fingers, and I study the screen. It's a woman in a purple dress, a long braid down her back, her hands resting on her large belly, her head twisted around so her eyes can look at me through the screen. It's Charita. Pregnant.

"You know who that is?" she asks softly.

I nod. "You," I say. It's so weird that she can be in the screen and also sitting next to me. I know what pictures are. I understand how they work. But I've never been in the same room as a person and a picture who are the same people at the same time and also at different times.

"Yes," she says, taking her top hand off mine. I could move mine away from her now. But I don't. "But do you know who that is? Inside there?" Real-Charita's finger points to picture-Charita's swollen belly.

I shake my head.

"That's Jakey," she says. "Three years ago."

"Oh!" The word rushes out of me in a relieved breath. "When you say 'mother,'" I say, "you only mean the person you come out of."

Louis and Charita smile and bite their lips at once as if they can be happy and nervous at the same time.

"Well," Charita says. "That's the beginning of being a mother."

I start to get nervous again, but I ignore it and take a bite of hamburger. The food will distract me. The food will keep me from hearing anything I shouldn't hear.

That doesn't make sense because it's Liar's food.

"A mother is supposed to love, hug, laugh with, teach, and protect her children," Charita says, speaking to the delicious, meaty juice running down my chin.

The image of her hugging Elsie and Junior and Jakey all at once comes flooding into my mind like proof.

But Mother God created Charita and so how can Charita also be mother?

The words are swirling, jumping, rearranging in my heart and brain.

"Any other questions?" she says.

Too many. So many. They run like electric wires through my veins, tearing me to pieces. I won't let them out. I will squash Curiosity down below my throat, if I can't kill her altogether.

Forget the food. Forget the rich smells climbing into my nose and the steam from the spaghetti warming my skin. I can't hear all these awful lies about mothers and fathers. I can't let them take away my Ultimate Truths one word at a time.

I open my mouth. I'm going to do it. I'm going to ask to go home. Now.

But then, there's a new voice behind me at the table.

"Zylynn?" she says. I turn. I see her. My heart stops.

Jaycia.

"Close your books," Father Prophet said. "That's today's lesson." There were a whole bunch of new souls around so we saw him more those days: in the classrooms, the Chapel, the dorms. He was guest teaching our Light class.

Hermeel, the boy sitting in the desk in front of me, raised his hand. He was new to the compound still and always asking questions that the rest of us knew not to think of.

"If Mother God created the Light, and if we are the only ones who know about it . . . ," he began.

Father nodded, a smile on his fleshy face. He never minded questions if they were about Mother God and Light. Or if they were about following instructions. He never minded our questions unless they came from Curiosity.

"Why is there sunlight everywhere?" Hermeel concluded.

Father walked up the aisle of desks and put his big hand on Hermeel's cheek. "Mother God invites everyone into her Light. She wants everyone to abandon greed," he said. "She provides invitations, like sunlight, all over the world. It's a wonder that so many people choose to ignore her, isn't it?"

"But—" Hermeel said.

"Shh, now," Father Prophet said. He put his thick finger lightly on Hermeel's lips. "You are about to wander into danger. Why should you think about sunlight on the Outside when Mother God has blessed us with so much Light here Inside?"

Hermeel sat frozen.

"Curiosity is the greatest evil, Hermeel. Do not invite her into my classroom." Father slowly removed his hand from Hermeel's face. "Can anyone give Hermeel an example of a safe question?"

My hand was in the air. I could hardly believe it. But I had been thinking about her all day and I had to know the answer.

Father raised his bushy gray eyebrows at me. It was unusual for anyone who wasn't new to ask questions. "Y-yes, Zy-Zylynn?" he said, almost like he didn't quite remember my name. Which was silly, he loved my name.

"Now what happens?" I said.

He lowered his eyebrows. "Yes, that is a safe question. Perfect. As you know, now you go to Exercise, just like every day," he said.

"Th-that's . . . that's not what I meant," I said.

Father froze in the space between Hermeel's desk and mine. His eyes darted between our two blond heads. I could feel everyone in the room holding their breath. There was no rule about correcting Father Prophet but we'd never heard anyone do it.

"OK, Zylynn," Father Prophet said. He put that note in his voice that told us he was trying for patience. The note that was always there when he reminded us about how we were from the Darkness and could never understand everything about Mother God the way he could.

I made the words rush out of my mouth. I didn't think they came from Curiosity. It was a question about what had happened here, Inside. "Now what happens to Jaycia?" I asked.

I felt the other kids swivel in their chairs, turning their heads and bodies to study my face.

Someone said, "Who?"

Father Prophet froze and stared at me, so I kept talking.

"It was her thirteenth birthday yesterday," I say. "She wasn't here, she didn't get a ceremony. What will happen to her?"

His eyes were huge now, like they were trying to escape the layers of skin piled up around them on his face. Still, he didn't answer. We sat like that for a long time, everyone staring at me and staring at me and it felt like their eyes were squeezing my heart inside my chest but I needed to know the answer so I sat and waited.

"Can anyone else tell Zylynn what will happen to a boy or girl who is not here when he or she turns thirteen?" Father Prophet said.

Hands went up around the room, eager to please him.

"If the girl turned thirteen yesterday and she wasn't here, she's stuck," Atkeesa said.

"She would dissolve into the Darkness forever; she will

always be tortured," Sunuko said.

My head was shaking, shaking, shaking back and forth. My brain was a swarm of moths flapping in my ears. She'd been gone only days or weeks: none of them remembered her. Did even Father Prophet forget Jaycia?

"Good job," Father said. He made an indication with his arm that all of us could get up and move on to Exercise, but he put his big hand tight on my shoulder and kept it there as he led me into the sunshine.

When we were alone outside the classroom, he froze with me stuck beneath his palm. He bent over my ear and hissed, "I will tell you the truth, if you think you are ready for it. Are you?"

I nodded.

"You love me, right? You love me more than anyone, more than Jaycia?"

She was my friend. Except I couldn't say that, I couldn't say "my." I nodded.

"This truth is not sad. If you are able to let out the dark greediness, you'll see it as fact and you'll move closer to the Light. It's not a bad truth."

I nodded harder now. My shoulders relaxed under his grasp. The truth was not bad.

"She has forgotten us," he said. "You must forget her too."

I swallowed.

"She's doomed," he said. He shrugged. "She has chosen to be doomed. It's a fact of life. She will awaken in anguish every day, she will sleep in terror every night. She will be tortured by the Darkness for every second. Because she chose to believe the Liars. She chose to stay where the Light cannot save her."

My eyes were wide. My heart was pumping extra hard. I was scared for her.

"But it doesn't matter to you, right?" Father Prophet demanded. He didn't give me a second to reply, a second to think. "Anyone who is not here does not matter to you. Remember that, Zylynn. Remember that or you will be in danger. And I do not want there to be danger between you and me."

He stared at me so hard, his big face was feet above mine but it felt like it was pressing into me anyway. A jiggle started in my heart and I knew it was fear even though I couldn't be afraid because underneath Father's gaze was the safest possible place to be. Still, with his face staring down on me and his hand squeezing my shoulder, I started to shake.

Then, with a swish of his white cape, he turned and plodded away from me, the red dust of the path climbing onto the cuffs of his white pants and the hem of his cape. I only watched a second before I hurried to catch up with the other kids who were scooting off in the opposite direction. I kept behind them though, so they wouldn't see me shaking.

Because Jaycia was in the Darkness forever, but I thought I might love her anyway. And that didn't seem like something I could tell anyone, ever.

Fourteen

"OH MY GOD. OH MY GOD, oh my God," Jaycia is saying behind me. I turn to Louis and Charita. I'm frozen, shocked. Louis and Charita are too. Their mouths hang open and they stare at her.

It can't be her because the girl behind me is happy and talking and in a restaurant, which is a place full of food. It can't be her because Jaycia is doomed.

"I'm sorry, I'm sorry. I mean, 'oh my goodness.'" She giggles and it breaks the spell.

That's her laugh.

It's really her.

I turn my head and look up at her.

She looks mostly the same. Her eyes are a little brighter. Her hair is a little longer. Her body is a little thicker. Healthier.

She looks OK.

Totally un-tortured.

"Jaycia," I say. "Hi."

She puts her hands under my arms and drags me out of my seat. Then she throws her arms around me.

I've never been hugged by a kid before. But now Jaycia is here and she's alive and she's OK and she's hugging me. Her arms knock the shock right off my shoulders and what's left is . . . relief. Happiness.

I hug her back. We squeeze each other. Then she starts dancing around a little and she's laughing and I still can't do that but I smile. And I'm happy.

"You're OK," I say, when the hug is over.

Jaycia's Abomination was my Abomination. But Jaycia is here in front of me. Jaycia is OK.

Jaycia squeals. "Oh my God, I thought they were never going to let you out of there! But you're here! You're really here."

I don't want to be here, Father. I promise. It's hard to mean it with Jaycia smiling at me like that.

"What does this mean? Is it over? Is he gone? Did they finally find out everything about the tea and the Hungry Days and all that?"

She's talking so fast and dancing around so much I can barely keep up with her words. I have no clue what she's talking about.

"Who is this, Zylynn?" Louis asks. His voice seems to come from far away, as if Jaycia and I were in our own invisible room and he's on the other side of the door.

I don't turn around. "This is—"

"Janice!" Jaycia cuts me off. "Please, please, please call me Janice now."

Charita stands and puts an arm around my shoulders. She stretches her other hand out to Jaycia and they shake hands like two Brothers. "I'm Charita. And this is Louis—" He stands too. "Zylynn's father."

And like that, I'm scared again. My head goes back and forth, back and forth, back and forth. *He's not my father. He's not my father. He's not my father.*

"Oh, Zylynn," Jaycia almost-whispers. "You're still so confused." Then her arms are back around me but it's not a happy hug this time. I don't reach up to hug her back.

She's OK.

But she's stuck in Darkness.

How can that be?

"You're going to figure it out, all right? It'll be scary but you'll figure it out and then everything will be better. Believe me," Jaycia says. "That's how it happened for my mom too. And you weren't in as deep as her. You weren't in as deep as a lot of people." She lets go of me and looks at Charita and Louis. "She really wasn't," Jaycia says. "Zylynn was the only one who ever asked questions. She was the only one who let me laugh."

I can't stand the talk of fathers and mothers and the other things Jaycia is saying that I don't understand. Things that make it seem like I'll have to choose between her and Light, between love and safety, something I don't think I can do.

"I . . . I saw you. In Target," I say.

"Really? On Thursday?"

I nod.

"You really did," Charita whispers.

"I was there that day! You did see me! Where were you?"

"Oh my gosh," a new voice says. I look up, and standing next to Jaycia is Marmelon, one of the women who used to be at the feasts, who used to be a Gatherer. Her hair is long and gray and tied up behind her head like it was the last time I saw her. But she's not wearing the long white skirt anymore. She's not crying or sighing. She's smiling. She barely looks like her old self. "Zylynn. Would you look at that, Janice? It's Zylynn. She got out!"

They're both laughing and laughing but I'm getting more and more scared.

What happened to Jaycia? Why does she have a new name? Why is she here with Marmelon? Why is she laughing so much when she's supposed to be tortured every day?

Charita says, "You must be Janice's mother?"

"Sure am," Marmelon says. Even though she knows better. Or used to know better.

"And you were at the compound too?" Charita asks.

Marmelon puts a hand on Jaycia's spiky hair and shifts it back and forth. I wonder, for a second, what it would feel like if Charita did that to my hair.

But, no. That's not what I wonder. I wonder how I can get back Inside.

It may look like Jaycia's OK, but she's not. I should know that. I have to trust Father Prophet. She must be being tortured in some way I can't see, can't understand yet. Marmelon too.

"I'm not proud of it but I got us roped in," Marmelon is saying. "I just—I was having a hard time, you know? And I met a Gatherer. And everything she said seemed to make sense. The promise of freedom and no decisions to make . . . it was too much for me right then."

"It can happen to anyone," Louis says.

"Yes. I thought, this! This is how I can keep my baby girl safe. But the next thing I knew, it was like I couldn't think for myself anymore."

Louis and Charita are nodding.

"Janice got us out though. She never fell for it. She's got a brain of steel, my girl."

So many *mys*. So many times so many people are breaking the Ultimate Truth here: *my mother, your father, my girl.*

Charita says, "Why don't we talk over here and let these two catch up?"

And then it's just me and Jaycia sitting at the table. And suddenly it's like the middle of the night when it was only the two of us awake no matter how loud she was being. Suddenly it's private. I'm back in friendship.

Jaycia laughs again. My friend.

Even I'm breaking the Ultimate Truth, out here in the Darkness. It's terrifying.

I'm still going to love her even if she's stuck in the Darkness. I think Mother God would be OK with that.

"When did you get out?" Jaycia asks. "How did you get out? How are you? They seem nice. Do you like them?" The string of questions flows easily from her mouth, each accented with a hint of a giggle.

"How are you so happy?" I ask. "You know you're stuck here forever, right? You're stuck in the Darkness and you'll be tortured every night and—"

"No," Jaycia says. She tries to keep talking but I don't let her.

"Let's go back, OK?" I beg. "I know what we did was really wrong. It was terrible. And I know you're already thirteen but maybe we can beg Father to forgive you and then you won't be stuck in the Darkness anymore?"

Jaycia puts her hand on my shoulder to stop me from talking. She shakes her head. "We didn't do anything wrong, Zylynn."

"But the Abomination—"

She cuts me off. "We didn't do anything wrong." Her head is still shaking. Her hand is still on my shoulder.

"The cheese," I hiss. It's so awful I can barely admit it, even though Jaycia was there with me.

"We didn't do anything wrong," Jaycia says, a little too loudly. Almost like she's angry now.

"We stole that cheese," I argue. "We stole it and then we ate on a Hungry Day."

Jaycia slaps her thigh, her eyes are dark now. "They were starving us," she says. "Don't you get that? They were killing us."

"Please," I whisper. "Please. Let's go back. Let's go home." I pretend I can't see how her head is shaking. "I don't want you to be stuck in Darkness forever."

"I want to be here," she says quietly. "You'll figure it out, eventually. Then you'll want to be here too. I promise. Everything they told us Inside was a lie. Everything."

"No," I say. "The Liars are on the Outside."

Jaycia nods. "I know it's hard, Zylynn. It was your whole life. But it was all lies. Everything."

"No," I say again. Louder this time. There's no punishment for yelling here so I might as well.

"Ask Louis, Zylynn. Talk to your father about it."

"The Prophet is my Father!" I yell.

People are looking at us now. Jaycia isn't smiling or laughing anymore. She's ducking her head.

"The Prophet was a Liar and a thief," Jaycia says. "He took all of our money, mine and my mom's and everyone else's too. He tricked us, all of us. He's got your mother captured there still—"

"MY MOTHER IS GOD, MY MOTHER IS GOD, MY MOTHER IS GOD." I'm being so loud Charita and Louis and Marmelon rush toward us. Then I hiss, "You were there. You know the truth, Jaycia."

"God. Please don't call me that, OK?" Jaycia says.

"It's your name!" I wail. "Of course I'll call you that. That's what Father wanted!"

"No, Zylynn, look—"

I cut her off. I interrupt her. Something else I've never done. "It doesn't matter. I won't call you anything. I don't ever want to talk to you anyway. You were my friend but you turned your back on the Light and now you're just a no-good, evil, dirty Liar."

Jaycia has tears in her eyes now. Louis and Charita are right near us, but I can see Marmelon holding them back, whispering to them.

"It's never going to be over," my friend whispers.

"The Light will always win." I spit the words at her. "You know that."

Jaycia takes a shaky breath. She pulls a pencil from her pocket and scribbles on a napkin. "OK," she says. "Here's my phone number. In case you ever figure everything out and you need me."

Then she gets up and leaves.

There are ten numbers scribbled on the napkin. Under them is one word. *Janice.*

I'm crying hard as I clutch the napkin. So hard I let both Louis and Charita hug me when she's gone.

The Darkness did get Jaycia. I don't understand how it's torturing her, but it did worse.

It turned her into a Liar.

* * *

I'm standing beneath my lightbulb in my room. No. *The* lightbulb in *the* room.

After Jaycia left, everyone in the restaurant was staring at us. Louis said we would take the food to go. We took it back to their kitchen in little white boxes and ate it there. I didn't get a chance to ask them to take me home. Charita tried to talk about what happened, about me yelling, while we ate lunch. But I didn't say anything, and then Louis said we didn't have to talk.

He said I can talk when I'm ready.

He doesn't know I'll never be ready.

I'll be gone. I'll be back Inside. And then I'll forget I ever yelled like that. I'll forget my old friend is stuck in Darkness. I'll forget that Jaycia is just another Liar now.

I have to pray before I go to sleep so I'm trying to make myself say the words I should and nothing else. Just the bedtime prayer. No extra words or thoughts. I'm trying not to talk to Mother because Father Prophet said not to. Because I need to get home. Because when I wake up I will only have three days left.

I can't make my brain be quiet. Curiosity is a tornado spinning in my skull and I can't make her stop. Is Charita really also a mother? Where's the person *I* came out of? Why is Charita giving hugs like that to the kids who came out of her and the person who I came out of is gone?

Is Louis really a father? What do they mean when they say he's my father?

Is Jaycia really a Liar?

If I pray while the questions run in circles, I'll ask them by accident. I'll ask them to Mother God. Then I will have done that terrible thing again.

The Liars keep asking me what I want to do, to wear, to eat, where I want to go. I only have to ask to go home.

Tessie.

I only want to learn a little bit more before I do.

I squint at the light, trying to make it blur like they do if I stare into the lightbulbs next to the bunks Inside for too long. But it's too weak.

Father Prophet will punish me for wanting answers. And for talking to Mother God. And for eating so much, wearing colors, liking Charita, calling Jaycia *my* friend out loud . . . I've committed so many Abominations he'll punish me right up to my ceremony.

The next time they ask, I promise him, *I'll tell them to take me home.*

Tessie . . . Tessie . . . Tessie . . .

The word is bouncing in my skull all night.

Fifteen

ELSIE IS WALKING TURTLE AROUND MY room again. The morning light is streaming in through the window.

"Hey, Zylynn," she says. "How old are you?"

"Twelve. Almost thirteen," I say.

I watch her as she moves Turtle over the desk, then she makes him walk on the wall like a bug. Then he climbs my leg until he's sitting in my lap and she's sitting at my feet.

"But you're barely bigger than me," she says.

"So?" I say.

"So. Twelve. That's old."

"How old are you?" I'm getting used to all of these questions coming out of my mouth. The Darkness keeps eating my words.

"Five," she says. "Junior's seven and Jakey's three. Except Jakey will be four soon and then I'll be six. When's your birthday?"

"Wednesday," I say.

She shoots up on to her feet and puts her little hands on my shoulders. "Wednesday like the next Wednesday that's coming? Like the next time it's Wednesday it'll be your birthday?" She's jumping up and down. I don't know why she's so excited. It's not her ceremony. She won't even be there.

Unless I can figure out a way to take her with me.

I nod.

"And today is Sunday," Elsie squeals.

I nod again.

"How many days till Wednesday?" she asks.

"Three," I say.

"Three days! We're gonna have a party!" she yells. "Party! Party! Party!"

> **Party** (n.): a social gathering of invited guests to one's home or elsewhere for purpose of conversation, refreshment, entertainment, etc.

"No," I say. "I won't have a party. I'll have a ceremony."

"Oh," she says. "Cool."

If I take her with me, if I make her a new soul, Father will be so happy with me. I won't be hit or hungry.

I take a deep breath. "Do you . . . ," I say. "Do you . . . do you want to come? With me? To my ceremony."

"Sure!" Elsie cheers.

And I smile so big. So huge.

* * *

After lunch, Charita says, "Come on into the living room, guys. I want to show you something."

Guys is Junior, Elsie, Jakey, and sometimes Louis. It's another one of those code words like *honey* and *babe* and *Dad*.

The kids all get up from the table, leaving their plates at their seats. I stare at them. I can't believe that they do this all the time. Crusts and orange slices and an inch of milk: they leave so much behind. It's like they've never been hungry.

My own plate is in front of me where I sit at the table. It's empty. But I'm not hungry enough to eat the peanut butter crusts off Jakey's plate. I get itchy. This is the first time I've ever been alone in the kitchen.

I wonder how big that fridge can actually be. I wonder how much food I would see if I opened the door.

I stand and tiptoe a few steps before I hear Charita call my name. "Zylynn? Would you bring me my water?"

I freeze. Did she see me somehow? Is opening the fridge here a Mistake? An Abomination?

I haven't been punished, yet, but I know there are punishments in Darkness. Punishments worse than Hungry Days or pingings or anything I could even imagine when I was in the Light. I'm sure of it.

I don't touch the fridge.

Charita's glass of water is on the counter. I pick it up and go into the living room. The kids and Charita and Louis are all sitting on the floor around the low table. They call it a *coffee table* even though it never has any mugs on it.

There are six huge, shiny books on the table between them. They're all looking through them, smiling, pointing, talking, squealing, laughing.

"Thanks, Zylynn," Charita says.

I turn to go. I'm not sure if I'm supposed to be here or not. I don't belong. I don't want to belong.

But what are they looking at? How come they can laugh and we can't?

Charita grabs my wrist and tugs it lightly. "Do you want to see this, Zylynn?" She points at one of the books. It's full of pictures, a photo album. I've never seen one before. "That's Elsie as a baby," she says. I look at Elsie as a five-year-old, then Elsie as a baby. They don't look too much alike. Elsie as a five-year-old has braids and green eyes and a crooked front tooth. Elsie as a baby looks like a bald raisin. It's weird to be able to see two of her at once.

I point to the picture next to her. "Is that one Jakey or Junior?" I ask.

Charita laughs. "That's Elsie too. In the hospital, one day old."

Hospital (n.): an institution in which sick or injured persons are given medical or surgical treatment

I gasp. "Why was she in the hospital?"

Charita turns to smile at me. "Just to be born," she says.

She starts flipping pages in the book. "There she is at a month old." Elsie, the real one, comes to stand behind Charita's other shoulder. Charita keeps flipping pages. Junior and Jakey and Louis stare at the other books, mumbling and giggling every once in a while.

Charita says, "There she is at six months, see that big smile?"

I nod, even though Charita can't see me. It looks a little more like Elsie now with tufts of her hair and greener eyes.

"Here we are at the zoo," she says. "And the park. The library." She squeezes Elsie's hand. "Here's your first birthday party!"

This picture is stuffed with people and I have to squint at it to find baby Elsie, but she's in it, pulling Charita's hair. Yeah, there's a younger version of Charita there, and Louis next to her, Junior on his shoulders. And behind him are the two gray people from yesterday, only not as gray. And next to him—

"That's Uncle Alan," I blurt. "But with hair."

Elsie giggles. "Now he's bald."

Charita pats her leg. "Elsie, honey, that's not nice," she says. I stare at Uncle Alan and his hair. Short. Yellow. Clumpy against pale skin. Just like mine.

"Why does his hair look like mine?" I ask.

Now Charita's head turns back to me quick-quick. Her smile is so huge. "You noticed that, huh? It's because he's your uncle. Just like—did you notice that Elsie and Junior and Jakey and Louis all have green eyes like you?"

"Yeah," I say.

"Well, that's because they're your brothers and sister and you are Louis's daughter."

Questions flood my brain. Curiosity rubs her furry body up and down my legs making me squirm. But I keep them there in my skull. If I ask her more about the green eyes, she'll say that thing about Louis again. And I don't want to hear it. I don't want to start yelling like I did yesterday, not in front of Elsie.

I need Elsie to want to come back with me. I can't scare her.

Charita turns a few more pages and we watch Elsie stretch into a three- four- five-year old. Then she flips the book closed. On the front there is a piece of tape with *ELSIE* printed on it.

"That was fun," Charita says. "Now who wants ice cream outside?"

Elsie, Junior, and Jakey all start screaming in that weird way that screaming can be happy. I've figured out that their "outside" means "in the air."

And now I know that strawberry ice cream is cold and smooth and sugary and filly-up and delicious.

It's later in the day, right before dinner, and Charita is herding us through the kitchen to go upstairs and wash our hands. The photo albums are still on the coffee table. Six big bound-up books. Six strips of tape. I only glance at the one closest to the stairs.

ZYLYNN.

* * *

"Perhaps you are curious," Father Prophet said. "Perhaps you wonder this or ponder that."

In Chapel. Hard stone against my back, cold on the back of my arms. Jaycia sitting too close to me. Humming softly.

"Perhaps you think you'd like to experience, see, taste, or feel what cannot be found here Inside."

Jaycia stopped humming and stared at Father, hard. Her fingers gripped the edge of the stone bench until her hands turned red.

"Perhaps you think you cannot help it when Curiosity, conniving seductress that she is, climbs into your soul and orders you to test the Darkness out, to play with the edges of your Light, to ask the questions. It is hard for you; I know. I am compassionate to all of you who are born of Darkness and greed and the Outside. I understand Curiosity can be a powerful force."

I thought Jaycia might rip the skin over her knuckles, the way she was clutching the edge of the bench.

"But remember this: The Light is more powerful than any force."

He paused. The lights shined off every inch of his white pants and shirt and cape. I knew to my bones that Curiosity would never get to me. Father would always keep me safe.

"If you do succumb to the traitorous vixen that is Curiosity, if you do not try hard enough to summon your Light and cast her out, then you are responsible for all of the pain that will befall us this week, this month, ever. Curiosity is the most cunning disguise of Darkness."

Jaycia was shaking, but only I could tell.

I worried for her. I worried that Curiosity had gotten her already.

It's the middle of the night. I stand in the open doorway of the Pink Stripes Room and stare out. The hallway is dark. Pitch-dark. If I step into it, if I let Curiosity make that choice for me, my skin will burn. My hair will fall out. My face will contort. I'll be marked forever.

She is wires wrapped around my rib cage, pulling me forward, pulling me into the night.

The last time I left my bed in the middle of the night, I was cast into Darkness.

I make the same promise I made last night. I'll tell them to take me home. They'll ask what I want to do again. And then I'll say it.

Curiosity yanks and I'm standing in the black. The Darkness. Except there's a puddle of light climbing up the stairs. I move toward it. The light in the living room is on.

I feel more alone in the living room than I do in the Pink Stripes Room. It's lonelier to be somewhere that's usually full of people.

There are sounds around me: the dishwasher in the kitchen, the creak of a floorboard over my head. But they aren't human sounds. I glance over my shoulder to make sure Charita and Louis and everyone else stayed where they sleep and didn't follow me and don't know I'm here because I don't want them to know that I want to know what they maybe do or maybe don't want me to know.

I'm only going to look at the cover of the book. The tape. I'm not going to open it.

I was right. The black letters are bold against the white tape in the living room light: *ZYLYNN.*

There's *ELSIE, JUNIOR, JAKEY, VACATIONS, JUST THE TWO OF US.* And *ZYLYNN.*

Curiosity has her fingers pulling my hair, her palms pushing my back, her elbows nudging my shoulder blades. I move forward, away from the right direction, away from the Pink Stripes Room, away from the Light, until I plop on the leather couch.

It squeaks under my pajamas. I jump. I look back toward the stairs and freeze for minutes or hours.

No one's there. I'm still all alone.

Is the *ZYLYNN* from the book cover me? Could there be another Zylynn? I want to check that. That's all.

I lean forward, slip my palm beneath the cover of the Zylynn book, and flip it over so the back side is up. In case it is me. I'll only look at the recent ones. The ones where I look like me now. It won't be as creepy if I don't look like two people when I'm really only one.

There are a bunch of blank pages in the back of the book and Curiosity motors my fingers as I flip through them.

There's only one picture on the first filled-out page I find.

It's me. It's seven-days-ago me. I'm tiny, far away from wherever the camera was taking the picture. Brother Chansayzar is on my left, Brother Wrinkesley is on my right. They wear creased white pants and linen shirts with white buttons down the front and on the shoulders—the Officials of the Light. The most important Brothers, the closest to Father Prophet. They each have a hand on one of my elbows. I'm a speck between them.

Those whitewashed bricks are behind us. We're standing outside the compound.

I figure it out. The picture was taken one minute before they put me into Louis's car. It was taken right after I was forced out the gate. Right after they took me by the shoulders and told me nothing.

It was my first moment in Darkness. I was terrified.

I lean over the coffee table until my nose is almost touching the glossy page. I study myself in the picture. My hair is sticking up in weird angles, pasted to my ears and forehead in big chunks. I run a finger through my real hair, my now hair. It's smooth. It's getting used to shampoos. I bring my hand down to my cheek. I feel the way I can push a finger into it next to my lips. There's skin there. Something there. The girl in the picture is so skinny her cheeks collapse between her jaws.

Her eyes are blank. She looks dead.

The camera was wrong. I wasn't dead. I was too scared to look that dead.

My heart bounces in my chest.

I flip the page. I don't find another picture at first. Instead, the next few pages I look at are articles on paper, the way Charita showed me you could use Google to look up articles about anything. They're printed out and sealed beneath the plastic. The first one says *Prophet or Profit?* The next one says *It Happened to Me; It Could Happen to Anyone.* The next one says *Doctor Flees with Horror Stories.* What do these have to do with the tape: *ZYLYNN*?

I want to read them. I want to know what they mean. But I'm wondering if Louis and Charita put this book here on purpose. If they want me to read them. If they've lured me down here with the promise of pictures to trick me into reading a whole bunch of lies about where I come from.

So I flip through without reading another word.

After pages and pages and pages there's a picture again.

It's a girl. A small one. She's sitting on a sandy floor, looking up. Her eyes are green.

It's me. Little Me and Now Me are both in the room, like it went with Elsie earlier.

How old am I there? It's hard to tell because I'm sitting, but my hair is long, past my ears, so it must have been a few years ago. It must have been before Father mandated matching haircuts.

I had forgotten there was a time of long hair. But now I remember. Because of the picture. I'm probably not supposed to be remembering things.

There's a blue crayon in my little hand, but I don't have any paper. I am looking right at the camera, but I'm not smiling.

I stare at the picture so hard I almost don't see the note pasted next to it.

Louis

Everything is fine here. Please don't worry about us. You can see that Zylynn is beautiful and growing.

Me

Goose bumps climb to my elbows from where my fingertips rest on the picture. They snake up my arms and make a nest on the base of my neck. I glance up the stairs. It's still dark up there.

I know I shouldn't, but Curiosity has control of my fingers. They turn the page.

I'm smaller in the next one. Barely able to reach the mattress of the bottom bunk that I'm leaning against. Maybe four or five years old. But I also look older than I did in the last picture, in some ways. My cheeks puff out. I'm smiling. There are rolls on my stomach and you can see them because my shirt is too small, riding up on my back. And my shorts . . . they're green. I thought I'd never worn a color until I got here.

Louis,

Here's Zylynn on her sixth birthday. Just in case you care. Just in case you decide to come back into the Light to be saved with your daughter.

Me

Daughter.

The next picture. On my fifth birthday, I'm wearing blue overalls and a gray T-shirt. My smile is even bigger. I'm sitting at a table with a huge bowl of ice cream in front of me.

Why don't I remember colors or ice cream or smiles?

Louis,

I cannot believe we haven't seen you for a year. Please come back. It's not too late for you to come back here and be a part of the Movement. I don't want to lose you.

Me

On my fourth birthday there are two pictures. I'm wearing a pink dress. A dress. Who knew I ever wore a dress? In one of the pictures I'm alone, fat, smiling. I don't know how I know it's me, but I do.

In the other, there are people in the picture, so many. I recognize Itheera and Morthasia and Wontansia and Brother Malcomen and Brother Tomlinkin and Brother Carpalyle and Thesmerelda and Taneely. There are oodles and oodles of people who crowd into the picture, some of them I know have disappeared and I can't remember their names and their faces are fuzzy in my mind. Others I forget all the way. What are they all doing in the picture? Why do we all look so happy? Why are we even gathered for my birthday? I was only four, not thirteen.

Then, in the middle of the picture, I see him. He looks different, but it's him. His gray eyes. His cape. His face is skinny. Four-year-old me is in his arms: Father Prophet.

It's hard to read the note with the tears in my eyes.

Louis,

I don't understand why you left Zylynn and me. The Movement needs you. Remember he has always said from the beginning that if we are going to paint the world Light, we have to do it all the way. Commitment, he said. We have to block out greed. You'll get addicted to it again. I'm so worried about you.

Father says there are so many things to fear out there: greed, drugs, guns, Curiosity.

I know I left last month, but I left for the mission. I left for the Movement. I was being obedient to the Light. I didn't leave like you did. I'm afraid for you. You need to return and cast the Darkness out. I'll be here waiting for you.

Me

Who is *Me*?

That's the end of the notes. After that there are pages and pages of pictures. Of me. I'm a toddler doing toddler things. Playing with a big plastic truck. Drawing on the walls with a crayon. Hugging some lady's leg. You can't see her head in the picture. There are ones of me and Louis. I know it's him. He's not so wrinkled and his fur is not so gray but his eyes are green and his face is kind and it's the same shape and it's him. He's kissing my cheek, throwing me in the air, handing me a big bowl of ice cream.

He knew me.

He was there.

He was Inside.

I look at the pictures slowly, tracing my finger over myself in each one. The whole book is backward from how it's supposed to be, from how Elsie's was. I'm getting fatter, bigger, more normal-looking as I get younger and younger. I trace my fat rolls, my smiles, my yellow hair, the colors of my clothes. I turn pages until I'm not a toddler anymore. I'm a baby doing baby things: sucking my thumb, smiling without any teeth, smearing food all over my hair. I turn and turn the pages until I really do get small and then I get bald and then I look like a raisin like Elsie did. And I know that picture is coming now, the one that was of Elsie in Charita's arms all wrapped up in a blanket and I turn pages faster because I wonder if I'm going to be in Charita's arms too and I think I want to see that because I think that if Louis and Charita both knew me, if they knew me longer than I've even known myself, maybe I can make everything make sense, maybe they aren't Liars, maybe they aren't part of the Darkness at all. Maybe Father has some plan. I want to see what Charita looked like all young and I want to see me all snuggled up in her arms and I want to try to remember what that felt like back when I was that tiny and when I didn't know that I should be afraid of her and when I didn't know what hungry was.

I turn the page. And then *bam*.

I see that picture. I jump. I slam the book closed. I whisper a scream.

It was me. It was me bundled up in a blanket looking like a shaved rodent with a head too big and a face full of wrinkles. But the woman holding me was not Charita.

It was Thesmerelda.

I left Brother Tomlinkin's with a note. He scribbled it out, frowning at me, and said, "Here, give this to your Exercise Coach today."

I was walking back across the angled path of the third circle. I wasn't thinking about the way Brother Tomlinkin frowned or the way he asked if I was only eight or even how long it had been since we'd seen the women and had a real feast. I wasn't thinking anything because I was obedient.

Footsteps came plunking behind me. Bare feet clapping against the clay quick, quick, quick like someone was chasing me.

"Zylynn," she said.

I turned my head. I saw Thesmerelda standing a foot behind me, maybe more. I made my hand move in an arc.

In my bones, I was scared. The women were still away. We hadn't had a feast and they hadn't squeezed and rocked us and we weren't supposed to see them again for a while. What was she doing here?

I kept walking. "Zylynn, wait. Wait, Zylynn!"

You will not see the women until the next feast. You may not talk to each other while walking on the clay paths. You must listen and obey anyone who is older than you.

Which rule was I supposed to follow?

I froze. I looked at her.

Gray hair twisted around her head like a wreath; her long white skirt picked up the pink dust from the ground; the white shirt slipped off her shoulder. I stared.

I remembered the night of the orange and the banana. I wondered if this was some sort of magical person Mother God had placed on the compound. I wondered if she was magical like this for only me or for all of the girls and boys.

"Where are you going?" she said.

I held up my note. "Exercise."

She nodded. Her mouth was twitching. Her eyes looked too wet. She opened her arms. "Zylynn, Zylynn," she said. "Come here."

I didn't move.

"I miss you. I miss my baby," Thesmerelda said.

I shook. I panicked. She said "my." She called me a baby. She called me hers even though I belong to Mother God alone.

I shook and shook and shook.

Father must be testing me, I thought.

I ran away.

Sixteen

THE SUNLIGHT DANCES ACROSS MY FACE, scratching at my eyeballs before I even open the lids. When I do, the sun is spilling through my window so much it drowns out the lightbulb on my ceiling. I roll toward the light, enjoying the way I can feel it warm on my arms, cutting through the air-conditioning that's always purring in their house.

And then I freeze. I bathed in the sunlight. I didn't look for the lights on the walls. I didn't listen for the Caretakers. I didn't wonder where the breathing of the girls sleeping around me had disappeared to.

It's the first morning I know exactly where I am before I open my eyes. It's the first night I haven't woken up panicked again and again and again.

I have to get out of here—now. Before the Darkness swallows me whole.

The house feels empty when I wander into the hallway in

pink shorts, a blue shirt, and green flip-flops. They slap my feet; they're so loud in the quiet hallway it makes me jump.

Have they left me here? Was looking at those pictures last night a Mistake? Am I in the real Darkness now? Am I alone?

There are three other doors, all of them are open, yawning into the hallway and begging me to cross the threshold and try to find the people: Louis or Charita or Elsie or Junior or Jakey. Why did no one knock this morning?

I walk into and out of the rooms. I see beds—one big, three little—with blankets heaped and twisted on top. I see toys strewn across the carpets in two of the rooms—plastic cars and trucks and huge LEGOs in one room, stuffed animals and coloring books in the other one. In the room with the big bed the carpet is empty but the rest of the furniture is covered with folders and papers and pens.

It's like Mother God plucked all of the people from this compound right in the middle of their lives. It's like, by opening that photo book, I cast them all even further from the Light and they will feel the sting of Darkness forever.

Should I care about that? Them?

My knees are shaking by the time I step down the stairs. I tiptoe past the coffee table. The photo books are gone, disappeared like all of the people in them. All of them except for me.

My flip-flops slap against the linoleum in the kitchen. It's empty. Is the food gone? I walk past the other kitchen door with the steps that lead to the family room, and approach the fridge. I hold the handle in my fingers, but I don't open it.

I shouldn't.

Curiosity has done all of this to me. I've failed to kill her. Curiosity is the opposite of Mother God. She is the end. She's the ultimate trickster. She is pure evil.

I should go back to my room and stand under my light and pray and pray and pray and pray to remember every individual hair on Father Prophet's head. I should sit at my window and make him walk down the street again. How long has it been since I did that? Two days? Three? How did I let myself get so tricked?

I need to find Louis and Charita. I need to make them take me home.

I release the handle of the fridge door.

I am alone.

I'm shaking so hard I can't move.

"Zylynn?"

I turn. Charita is standing in the doorway at the top of the stairs that lead to the family room. She's smiling.

My heart burrows comfortably into my chest. My hands stop shaking and lay at my sides. I tell my feet to stay. I'm close to rushing at her, hugging her.

"Hungry?" she asks. "How about some breakfast?"

That's not what I want her to ask. I want her to say what she's said before: "What do you want to do today?" I will tell her it's time for me to go home.

"Where is everyone?" I try.

She laughs. How does she do that?

"It's almost noon already! You had quite a sleep. I suppose it's good: teenagers are supposed to sleep into the afternoon. And you're almost a teenager, aren't you? The day after tomorrow, you turn thirteen!"

Oh yeah. She knows.

Ask me what I want to do today. Ask me.

"Elsie and Junior are at camp already. Jakey's downstairs playing on the tablet."

Ask me what I want to do.

"How about some breakfast?" she says again.

Just then, my stomach growls.

Guilty, I nod.

Later, I sit on the couch in the family room with the sun washing over my hair and I watch as Jakey drives a blue truck in circles on the carpet with his left hand. Charita sits at the desk with her computer.

Somehow she knows it's almost my birthday. Somehow she knows I'm almost thirteen. Somehow they always knew, even before I got here. Somehow they always knew me. This fact scratches the back of my brain.

Every once in a while Charita asks me a question. "Would you like to read a book, Zylynn?"

"No thanks." We don't read books. They're the breeding ground for Curiosity.

She goes back to clicking the keyboard that's connected to

the tablet like two of Junior's LEGOs.

"Would you like to go outside?"

"No thanks," I say.

Charita turns to look at me and sighs. "I know," she says. "It's so hot."

Jakey's hand drives the truck up my leg. It tickles.

I make a list of the questions I have. I keep them tucked into the folds of my brain.

Who is Tessie?

Why don't I remember Louis from when he was at the compound?

Why is Thesmerelda in Charita's book?

Is any of this real?

Once the questions are there, clear and black-and-white, I try to squeeze them into nothing and knock them one by one out my ears. I will not ask them. I will not be curious. I will not become a dirty, evil girl. I will not be like Jaycia. I will not become a Liar.

"I better start dinner," Charita says. "What's your favorite food, Zylynn? Do you have one yet?"

The sun is crawling down the sky already and she still hasn't asked the right question. Not once.

She wants to know my favorite food. She wants to give me computer games and books. She knows my birthday is coming. The facts slosh around my stomach making me sick. I can't figure out how these are lies.

I shake my head.

"Something new then?" she says.

I nod.

She hops up the stairs and Jakey follows her.

"You don't have to sit there, you know," Charita calls down from the kitchen. "You can read, go outside, play on the tablet. Whatever you want."

I want to go home. But she doesn't ask me.

Can I tell her anyway? Can I ask for something all on my own? Is a question like "will you take me home?" a bad one, a curious one?

I open my mouth to speak, but then she's gone.

I stand and wander over to the tablet. When I read the top of the screen, my jaw drops. It says:

Google Search: The Children Inside the Light

Charita has been reading about us. Us. I glance at the first few lines of blue text:

Wikipedia, the Free Encyclopedia: The Children Inside the Light

Official Website: The Children Inside the Light

The Tragic History of the Children Inside the Light

The Children Inside the Light—I Was Brainwashed

The Children Inside the Light: Be a Part of Our Movement

I race the little arrow of the mouse up and down the screen watching each set of blue letters go from thick blue to regular blue to thick blue. I want to click on every one. I want to read every article. I want to suck up all of the information, swallow it, and try to make everything make sense.

I recognize Curiosity. She's sitting on my shoulders again,

her icy hands wrapped around my neck. I try to shrug her off.

But this is different from the book last night. This time Charita was here reading these articles herself. She was trying to learn about us—me. For herself.

So she can't be using these to trick me. To lie.

I click on one of the articles.

The Tragic History of the Children Inside the Light

All of the ex-members of this group swear it started out innocently. They were hooked by the promise of a place without greed, a community to raise their children, childhoods with no pressure to be the best, with no unhealthy competition.

When Pastor Jim Levens left his home church and started the Children Inside the Light Movement back in 1995, he promised his followers a safe place. In the famous video he said, "I've found God. I've talked to her. God is a woman. God is our Mother." He claimed that God wants us to live in harmony and community and softness. He promised to provide his followers with everything God wants them to have if they were willing to come and live on his compound in the middle of the Arizona desert.

The video was passed from neighbor to neighbor across the southwest and people came from far and wide to meet the Prophet in the desert. Did he believe what he was preaching? Did he truly think he was the direct connection between all of humanity and its creator? Or was he only hungry for power and money? These are questions anyone familiar with the Children Inside the Light is apt to ask. But ultimately, the answer does not matter. The motivations of Pastor Jim Levens are unimportant when we consider the damage his actions

> have caused to hundreds of adults and hundreds of children.

I stop reading to think.

There's no one named Jim Levens on the compound. I've never heard a name like that before.

And the Children Inside the Light are the opposite of damaged.

I should stop reading. Part of me even wants to stop reading. But Curiosity has taken over. She forces my eyes back to the screen.

> For years, we Arizonians mostly ignored the white walls in the middle of the red sand. We described it as a "hippie commune." We brushed off the women who tried to tell us about the Light in parks or grocery stores. We didn't think about the Children Inside the Light when we went home to our nuclear families after our days in our capitalist jobs.
>
> That is until a man, Dr. Eli Thomas, fled the compound in the middle of the night with stories that chilled us to our bones. He spoke of malnourished children, of hundreds of people being punished by starvation, of zombies with no sense of individuality. He called Pastor Levens a crook: the price for admission to the Children Inside the Light is one's entire savings account and all worldly possessions including cars, houses, and land.
>
> Authorities are still perplexed as to how to handle this cult in the desert. The situation is similar to other cults that persist despite the rampant rumors of child abuse, violence, and brainwashing, such as the polygamists in Colorado City. State officials have visited the Children Inside the Light and found no indications of abuse clear

enough to shut it down or even to remove children whose parents insist they stay. Pastor Levens, of course, claims that individuals choose to stay on the compound and are protected by their First Amendment rights.

As usual, in Arizona, it's easier to pretend we don't see the fence in the desert than it is to admit children are being hurt right under our noses every day.

The article is lying.

Obviously. I'm Outside so everything is lying. I don't even have to wonder if it's true. I don't know who Pastor Jim Levens is. Or Eli Thomas. No one Inside had names like that.

But the Hungry Days part was true. It's weird to see them written about like that. Like whoever wrote this is angry that we were punished by not having food. Like food is a right, is as essential as Light. Or more essential than Light.

Is it? Does food matter more than Light?

I hit the back arrow so that the screen shows the list of articles again. I run the mouse over them again. I want to read another one. But I shouldn't. Curiosity is everywhere. And reading feeds her.

I'm about to hit the *X* at the top of the screen when I see the little orange box in the corner. It's a drawing with lines running in every direction and a blue circle right in the middle with a little arrow pointing to it. The words next to the arrow are black and bold and sure: **The Children Inside the Light Compound**.

I know what this is.

Map (n.): a representation, usually on a flat surface, as of the features of an area of the earth, showing them in their respective forms, sizes, and relationship according to some convention of representation

I click on the orange square and it spreads to the whole screen and morphs into a photograph. There it is. Safety. My home.

This is not a lie.

The entire thing is pictured on the screen from a bird's-eye view. The whitewashed buildings long and flat or tall and curvy or short and squat. The red-clay paths spiderwebbing between them. The three circles, each one more important than the one before. The exercise fields at the west end. Father Prophet's building at the north boundary. The stone Chapel rising up right in the center. I use the arrows on the side of the screen to zoom in on different parts, to move my compound right and left and up and down. The compound. Our compound. Her compound. Whatever. There are people on the paths, frozen into the computer screen, but I can't zoom in close enough to see who they are. I study the silver roofs of the Girls' Dorm and the Boys' Dorm and the Dining Hall and the classroom and the Teen Dorms and the Men's Dorm. I stare at it until it becomes a red-and-tan-and-silver-and-white blob that won't make any sense through the wetness in my eyes.

Tears (n.): fluid appearing in or flowing from the eye as the result of an emotion, especially grief

"Zylynn," Charita calls after I've been crying at the tablet for hours and hours. Or minutes and minutes. Some amount of time. "Elsie and Junior are home. Come eat some dinner."

I blink and blink and blink at the bright screen, trying to make my eyes dry, to make them look normal. I blink so hard I almost miss the little box on the side of the map. It's tiny but I'm sure I'm seeing the words right.

Get Directions.

I click on it and there it is. The map now has a bold line. There are two little circles, one labeled **Current Location** and the other labeled **The Children Inside the Light Compound**. Below there's a list of step-by-step directions to get me from Louis and Charita and Elsie and Jakey and Junior's house all the way home. And, at the very bottom of the screen, there's a little box that says **Print**.

Thank you, thank you. I'm coming home.

We eat dinner. The chatter of the Outsiders fills the kitchen but I stop listening to it.

They feed me and smile at me and give me colors and toys. They know when my birthday is. But this is Darkness. There's a link missing in the chain in my brain. Why is the Darkness so pleasant and soft and full of food?

After dinner, Elsie asks for ice cream. Junior and Jakey ask for cookies.

I take gulp after gulp of water trying to erase the spicy, delicious flavor of dinner from every crevice of my tongue. I have to forget it. I'm going to have to forget everything once I'm home: I should start now. Charita said we were eating something called tofu fajitas and when there was only one left, Louis let me have it. But that doesn't matter. I will forget about both of them soon.

"Zylynn?" Charita says. "Is there anything you'd like?"

She's standing at the freezer, the ice cream carton in one hand. Her head is turned so she can probably only sort of see me. Her hair is curly down her back.

When they stop cutting my hair will it be curly and black like hers? When I'm a woman will I look like her, smiley and curvy and soft? The women at the compound always had such hard lines. Why is that? Is Light harsh and Darkness soft? It feels like it should be the opposite.

I pry Curiosity's nails out of my arm again.

I open my mouth to say I'd like to go home when she restates the question: "Did you hear me? Any dessert for you, Zylynn? What would you like?"

Dessert. I wasn't even thinking about food. My stomach is comfortable, not protruding outward and making my skin stretch across my ribs, not collapsing inward and folding me in half. It's unnoticeable. It's so unnoticeable it's impossible not to notice.

"What would you like?" Charita says a third time.

I can't ask the question. Not now that it's night. I don't want to be in the black outdoors in the car. I don't want to have to walk Inside in the dark. I hate the night. Plus, Elsie and Junior and Jakey are watching me. The map makes it so I don't have to speak yet. The map is my gift from Mother God. The map is my last resort.

"A flashlight," I say.

Elsie giggles. "For dessert?"

I look at her. "No. Just to have it."

"Are you sure you don't want it for dessert?" Elsie sings.

She smiles through a mouthful of ice cream. The freckles on her cheeks punch out at me. Her green eyes are just like mine except extra shiny. I have the strangest urge to pinch her cheek right where her dimple is.

I shake my head. I smile. I don't think that it's good to smile out here, but when I look at goofy Elsie with the freckles and the sugary white cream on her little lips I can't help what the muscles in my cheeks do.

I'm going to take her with me. That'll make everything OK. For me. And for her.

"You're not going to eat the flashlight? Good," she says. "For a second I was afraid my new sister was a robot."

Junior and Jakey and Louis and Charita all laugh.

"Bee bop boo bop." Junior makes funny noises. "Feed me batteries."

"Beep-beep, boop-boop," Elsie says. She pokes me right in

the belly. “I must eat your flashlight.” She makes her voice flat. “I am Zylynn, the Flashlight-Eating Robot.”

She pokes me again right above the belly button. And the strangest thing happens. It starts at that point. A little bubble, a movement of my muscles. Not indigestion or cramps. Not painful. It bounces from my belly through my windpipe and it’s already out my mouth before I know what it is.

I laugh.

Seventeen

I TEST THE FLASHLIGHT IN MY room before I sneak downstairs. I turn it on and off forty or one hundred times. The light in it bounces off my gold carpet, weak but there under the burning lightbulb above me. I put on the pink whisper-clothes and I stand under the lightbulb but I don't say my prayer and I don't get into bed. I test the flashlight until the sink in the kitchen is no longer running and the footsteps are gone from the stairs and the hallway and the doors to the other rooms have stopped opening and closing.

On-Off-On-Off.

I keep it up while Louis's and Charita's voices sneak through the stripes in murmurs and muffled words.

On-Off-On-Off.

They really did give me a flashlight. All I did was ask, and here it is. And it works. Will it be that easy when I ask to go home tomorrow?

When the house around me has been still and dark and

sleeping for minutes or hours, I tiptoe to the door and creak it open. I don't hear any sounds. I wonder if this will be as easy as last night.

It'll be easier; I have the flashlight.

I switch it on and shine it into the dark hallway, watching the way Mother God battles the dark, the way it runs from every spot where the flashlight touches. The day after tomorrow, I will have the power of Light. I will light up the Chapel and I will be a part of Mother God forever.

I hold the flashlight in both hands, raise my arms, and point it straight down over my head. The dark can't get near me while I'm in this pool of light. I won't let it touch my skin. Not again.

The stairs are difficult but I manage to pad down them without even a toe brushing the dark.

The living room is dark tonight too and I slip right past it. But I do see that the *ZYLYNN* book is back on the coffee table. They left it for me. In the kitchen, the tile is cold on my bare feet. More stairs then, finally, I reach the family room. I flip the light switch and watch the whole room breathe a sigh of relief at the presence of Mother God.

Tomorrow or the next day, I'll be home.

In an instant I'm at the tablet and when I touch the mouse, my map still lights the screen.

It's one click. It's so easy. I'm so glad I learned how to do this in Computer Class on the compound.

Print.

VROOM! I jump.

The machine next to the computer sputters to life and clanks and shakes and clunks and makes so many noises. I'm sure I'm about to be caught by Louis or Charita or Curiosity in her ugly bodily form. I sit on the folding chair with my flashlight pointed to the stairs as if were a weapon that could protect me.

But nothing can protect me. I'm in Darkness. Even this flashlight might be a lie. Somehow.

The room falls back into silence, and I reach under and pull the paper into my hands.

Directions: Current Location (55 Apple Ct., Plainsville, AZ) to the Children Inside the Light Compound

The map is hot in my hands, the promises in this piece of paper running back and forth between my palms and fingers.

When I hit the little X above the map, the old screen appears.

Wikipedia, the Free Encyclopedia: The Children Inside the Light

Official Website: The Children Inside the Light

The Tragic History of the Children Inside the Light

The Children Inside the Light—I Was Brainwashed

The Children Inside the Light: Be a Part of Our Movement

All of these articles are probably lies, just like the one I read earlier.

Still, before I can help it, words come skipping into my brain uninvited.

Encyclopedia (n.): a book or set of books containing articles on various topics, usually in alphabetical arrangement, covering all branches of knowledge or, less commonly, all aspects of one subject

Tragic (adj.): extremely mournful, melancholy, or pathetic

Movement (n.): abundance of events or incidents

Others I can't find in there: *Website. Brainwashed.*

Even though I'm sitting in a bright room, I shine the flashlight over my head again, trying to banish Curiosity, to drown her. She has her hair wrapped all around my body now. She has her fingers in my mouth.

What do these things mean? How is our history tragic? And that word—*brainwashed*—it's so ugly, even without any meaning. Hair is for washing. And bodies and clothes. Not brains.

Since I can't beat Curiosity down, I go to Google the way Charita showed me. I'll distract myself with things I'm allowed to know. Words.

Daughter.

Wikipedia the Free Encyclopedia pops up saying, "A daughter is a female offspring; a girl, woman, or female animal in relation to her parents."

I am *daughter.*

Parents. The Wikipedia Free Encyclopedia says, "A parent

is a caretaker in the offspring of their own species."

Offspring: "In biology, offspring is the product of reproduction of a new organism produced by one or more parents."

By then I'm dizzy and tired and foggy and I don't care anymore. It's impossible to learn a new word, I decide, until you know all of the words. And you can't know all of the words until you learn new words.

Maybe that's how Mother God made Darkness so confusing.

But none of it matters anyway: tomorrow, when it's not nighttime anymore, I'll ask Charita and Louis to take me back to the Light.

And if they don't, I found my way.

Eighteen

I'M SITTING AT MY WINDOW STARING at the foggy gray outside again. My eyelids are heavy. They refused to close all night once I returned from the printer. My tongue is swollen from craving pomegranate tea. My eyes have been open for too many minutes and hours in the eight days I've been here.

Today is my last day as a child. I'm nothing but tired.

Maybe that's a part of how Mother God is punishing me.

I picture Father Prophet out the window, coming up the road.

"Tomorrow," I tell him. I whisper so close to the glass it makes streaks across my reflected face. "By tomorrow, I'll be back." This time, I know it's true. Today, I know I'll ask.

Even though I'm still dirty: Turtle is on my lap.

"Tomorrow," I repeat.

"Tomorrow is your birthday!" a small voice says behind me.

I whip my head around. Elsie stands in my doorway, balanced on her left foot. How much did she hear? What did I say out loud?

"Can I come in and play with you and Turtle?"

The noise plays in my head. The one from last night's dinner. The one I made. It came from me, my laugh. But it also kind of came from Elsie.

The laugh from dinner last night can't be mine because I can't have anything because I belong to someone else. But how can that laugh belong to Father when it started so deep inside of me?

Elsie has come into the room without me answering. She takes Turtle from my lap and climbs on to me herself, resting her back against my front. "What gifts did you ask for on your birthday, sis?" she says.

Sis is me. Short for *sister*. A nickname for a nickname. Another thing I'll never understand.

She twists to look at me, her freckles tickling the sides of my lips like sand stuck to my feet after a shower.

"I didn't," I say. I keep my mouth from smiling.

"Did you get presents for your last birthday?" she asks.

She yawns. I try not to like her warm body settling into mine. I try not to find that yawn adorable.

"Yes," I say. "Well, one."

"Only one?" she asks. "What was it?"

I close my eyes, remembering. "It was a square, a perfect cube, wrapped in purple paper. I got to open it in Chapel, in front of everyone."

"What was in it?" Elsie asks. She yawns again. She probably isn't paying attention. I keep talking.

"Under the purple paper, there was a white box."

"Uh-huh."

"And when I opened it, there was so much inside." My voice is hushed as I remember the glory of the moment. My heart had stopped. My eyes had gone wide. It was as if the box had contained her Light itself.

"Really?" Elsie turns around on my lap so that her knees are pressed into my hips. "Like toys? Books? Colored pencils?" She's fascinated. I should stop talking.

"A tomato. A big, big red one. A block of cheese. An apple and an orange. And . . . a chocolate bar." I'd stared at the box, then at Father, looking from his eyes back to my treasures over and over again. Father's smile was kind. I was sure I would never be hungry again. I had eaten the apple that day after our oatmeal dinner, and a few bites of the cheese. I had asked the Cooks to save the rest. And then . . . what happened to it? How did I forget it until now?

"That's it?" Elsie cries. "No ice cream? No toys? No cake?" She's screaming.

I shrug.

Something twists like a snake in my brain.

When I get home tomorrow, will they give me a gift? What if it's only fruit and cheese? How will I look at it with the same joy I did last year? How will I ever find joy again in oatmeal and apple slices . . .

I think I'm starting to figure out how these things in Darkness can be lies . . .

"Well, you are going to love your birthday tomorrow," Elsie

says. She turns back around and talks to Father out the window, even though I know she can't see him like I do. "Mom and Dad are the only parents I know who let us eat birthday cake for breakfast!"

I sigh.

"And wait till you get your presents! Even if you didn't ask for any, they will be so much better than a tomato! You don't have to wait till your birthday for a tomato, silly. You can have one anytime you want." I feel her giggles moving through her shirt against my stomach.

No. No. I won't be able to have a tomato anytime I want. No matter where I am.

After tomorrow I'll be stuck.

If they have me still in Darkness after I'm thirteen, if they rob me of my chance to ever be a full part of the Light, everything will stop—the food and the niceness and the strawberry shampoo and Turtle and all of the lies I wasn't supposed to be loving.

They used the food and the choices and the colors and the hugs and the softness to get me hooked, addicted. But if I get caught here forever, it will all stop. If I wake up here the day after my birthday, there won't be any food or colors or soft clothes to wear at night. There will only be stinging, burning darkness. And Louis and Charita will laugh and laugh at how stupid I was to let them trick me.

They'll laugh at me for being hungry. For being lonely. For being stuck.

That's how I'll learn to love oatmeal again. That's how I'll learn to love Inside. Because after tomorrow all of the choices out here would stop anyway.

Relief is ice in my veins. I've finally figured out the puzzle. They almost tricked me, but they didn't. And now I'll leave.

"Know what else?" Elsie asks.

"What?" My brain is still chewing on this new realization. I'm hardly hearing her voice or my own.

"We get to have cake after dinner too. Twice in one day. And everyone will sing to you and you'll blow out the candles and—"

"It's a lie, Elsie. It's all lies."

She freezes and twists to look up at me again. I'm not sure why I said it. I even said her name out loud. I'm not sure how I got so careless with my words. I used to count them. I used to worry about how much of myself, how much of my Light, I was leaving here in Darkness, how dim I would be when I get back.

The longer I'm here, the worse I get.

But it suddenly matters to me that this little girl knows the truth. If I can figure out how to take her with me, Father will forgive me more quickly. And if she's a part of the Light, I'll be allowed to love her like I'm starting to anyway.

"No," Elsie says quietly. "There's cake. We already bought the ingredients at the grocery store. I'm not lying. I promise."

Her lip trembles.

"I know," I say. "It's not you lying. It's the cake."

"Cakes don't even talk," she says.

"I won't be here tomorrow anyway," I blurt.

Elsie grips the chair at the sides of my legs. I feel all of her little muscles go tight.

"You don't have to be scared," I recite. Even though she does. She lives in Darkness. "It's time for me to go home. You can come with me."

"Where?" Elsie asks.

"You can come back with me. Back where I came from. You can be at my ceremony like you said you would, remember? You still want to come, right?"

Elsie is still nervous on my lap but she stays quiet, thinking. Finally she twists back to look at me again. "Just for your ceremony? Just for your birthday?" she says.

I don't know how to answer. I choose my words carefully. "My ceremony is tomorrow. It's my thirteenth birthday. I want to celebrate it with . . . old . . . friends. And you."

Elsie takes a deep breath and nods. "What about Mommy and Daddy?"

"Nope," I say. "Just with my sister."

Elsie smiles. She loves the word *sister.*

I try not to think about the fact that I used it to trick her. I try not to think about the fact that I had to use the word *my.*

"Then after the ceremony you'll take me back home?" she says.

And I try not to think about the fact that I'm a Liar too, now, when I nod.

"OK," she says. "OK. I'll come to your birthday party, Zylynn."

I don't bother to correct her that it's not a party. It's a ceremony. I can't tell her all the things I should, all the things I will know how to say after I spend the next seven years training to Gather.

"Don't tell Louis and Charita, OK? Don't tell anyone. Let this be our sister secret."

"'K," Elsie says. She scoots off my lap and starts playing with Turtle on the bed.

I look back out the window. The gray is gone. It's bright out. It's bright in my brain too. I understand now. The food, the colors, the soft words: they were more than lies. They were the punishment itself. I'll get home. Either today or tomorrow I'll finally get back to the Light. I'll be Inside, safe, when I turn thirteen and I'll stand in that Chapel and make the lights go on. But the Hungry Days will hurt so much worse after nine straight days of food. Wearing white day in and day out will be so boring it's painful. No hugs no smiles no nicknames no shampoo no turtles no playing no sister . . . nothing that is mine. It will hurt.

But not forever.

One thing I've learned from watching kid after kid join the Light: you only miss the Darkness until you forget it. And you always forget.

"Junior, take your brother and sister outside," Charita says after she collects our lunch plates. "Zylynn, Dad took a half day today. Louis. He's almost home. We'd like to chat with you for a few minutes if that's OK."

"Daddy's home?" Jakey squeals. "Already?"

"No fair!" Junior shouts. "Why just Zylynn?"

"Birthday stuff," Charita says. "Don't worry, you'll all get cake."

I almost don't hear them squeal. I feel Father's hand pressing gently on my shoulder. It's time.

We sit in the living room. I'm on the couch, my legs pulled into my chest so that Charita and Louis won't be able to see my heart beating through my shirt. The yellow one, like the sun in winter. Turtle is hiding in its folds. Five lunch strawberries settle cool into my stomach beneath him. I try to believe that I'm holding on to all of my favorite Outside things so that it will hurt even more when I let them go tomorrow. I try to believe I ate those strawberries to punish myself.

Charita is on the chair across from me tapping her foot on the floor and checking her watch every few seconds or minutes. It's weird how they have so little to do each day out here and yet they look at the time more and more.

Between us there's nothing but the coffee table and the *ZYLYNN* book.

Louis comes through the door and gives Charita a kiss on her lips and right in front of my eyes. The strawberries climb up the insides of my belly. He reaches out his palm like he's going to pat my head but I burrow myself further into the pillows and he falls heavily into the chair next to Charita.

"How are we today, Zylynn?" he asks.

Scared.

Father's fingers tighten on my shoulder, inch toward my neck.

I'll ask. Today. In this room. I promise.

The fingers stay on my skin, but they relax.

"Do you know why your dad would take a day off, Zylynn?"

I don't move. It's the wrong question.

"It's OK," Louis says. Those soft words wiggle into my ears and poke the Curiosity monster at the pit of my guts. "She wants to keep calling me Louis. That's OK."

I don't want to call you anything. I don't want to ever see you again.

"At home we do everything the same every day," I say.

Charita nods. "Do you want to tell us anything else about the Inside?" she asks.

I shake my head. All of my organs shake with it.

Make them ask the right question, Father. Make them.

"You know . . . ," Louis says, "you may have seen something in these photos or on Google that's difficult for you to understand. We thought you might want to read some articles or to look at the book together."

"It's good for you to hear about the place you come from. It's good for you to hear things from more people than just us," Charita says. "That's why we've left some things around for you to read and look at."

I knew they left those things for me on purpose!

Curiosity is all the way inside me, filling me up, twisting my guts together. Her tippy-toes balance on my hips, her breath spreads against the back of my throat. The book. It's full of so many questions. I'm full of so many questions. The answers are in front of me, sealed behind four silent lips. Staring me down. Daring me to ask.

If I ask the one question I should, I'll never get the rest of the answers.

"I thought we were going to talk about my birthday," I say. "It's tomorrow." Even though they already know. Liars always know the truth, sometimes more truth than I know about myself.

Louis sighs.

Charita pats his hand. "OK," she says. "What kind of cake? White or chocolate?"

My eyes widen. I've caught her in a lie. Finally. "Elsie says you already bought the ingredients."

Charita laughs.

Louis rubs his eyes.

"That little secret-squealer!" Charita says. "We did. We bought both kinds of cake mix."

The lies are a relief. They wash Curiosity back down.

"White cake."

I answer all of her lying questions.

Pink icing.

Cookie dough ice cream.

Yellow flip-flops. Pink shorts. A new toy so Turtle can have a friend.

The lies pile on top of the *ZYLYNN* book in the middle of the table and Louis and Charita think I don't notice. They think I'm stupid. After all these days they still think I'm stupid.

If I were still here tomorrow, I'd be stuck. There wouldn't be cake and ice cream and colors and toys. There would only be Darkness.

Louis's head is still down, his palm going back and forth against the base of his neck.

Finally Charita says, "And how would you like to celebrate? We can do whatever you like. It's your day."

Louis nods.

I stare at them wide-eyed and try to force the words from where they sleep in my chest. I've got them. She said we could do whatever I want. I want to go home. They'll either have to take me back Inside or they'll have to admit they're Liars. Either way, I win.

I'm not sure, then, why it feels like my heart is trembling.

"Do you have any ideas?" Charita says. "How do you want to celebrate thirteen?"

My eyes fall to my lap. *Speak. Speak. Speak.*

I don't look up. "My ceremony."

Louis's hand freezes on the side of his neck. Charita's teeth clack shut.

It's silent for minutes or hours. I look at them, finally.

"What's that?" Charita says.

Louis stares at me, his green eyes scratching into mine. "No."

"I want to go to my ceremony," I say, louder.

He stands, his eyes still scratching. "No."

I'm shouting now. "I want to go home. I want to go to the Chapel. I want to have my ceremony."

"There will be no ceremony." His voice is loud and heavy, weighing on my heart.

Red rage comes over my face, bathing the room in a delicious scarlet light. I'm so angry. I'm so relieved to finally be so angry. Water echoes in my ears. Liars. They are Liars.

Everything I've known to be true is true.

"You don't understand anything," I hear myself say but the voice is not mine. It's Elsie's or Jakey's when they don't get dessert. "You haven't been there in so long. You're a Liar now. You can't keep me from my ceremony!"

Red Louis and Red Charita go wavy in front of me. I'm seeing them through a flame. Father is painting them in truth, finally.

"You said I could do whatever I want! You just said that!"

"I know what we said, sweetie, but—" Charita's voice is so quiet.

Louis booms over her. "There. Will. Be. No. Ceremony."

The rage feels like it's all mine. Even though nothing can be.

You shouldn't be this angry, Father is saying. *You should have known this about them all along. You knew they were Liars.*

Louis is still talking—fast bullets of words I don't hear.

"I want to go home," my mouth cries.

Louis lunges at me, and this time when I flinch, he keeps moving forward. He stands above me with both of my wrists squeezed between his palms and his eyes lighting my hair on fire. "Listen to me, Zylynn. Really listen, OK? The ceremony is a lie. Inside, the whole thing is nothing but lies. Dangerous lies. They kept you hungry. They treated you badly. Think about how much healthier you are now. How much we will do for you. That's how a kid should be treated, OK? They were hurting you."

"No," I say. "No. I want to go back."

"Zylynn," Louis says. "No. You are never going back there again."

He drops my wrists and falls back into his chair. Charita is staring at me.

"Sorry," he says. "I shouldn't have scared you like that. But it's important for you to know. And it's true."

Relief rushes through me, whipping all remains of Curiosity out and far away. I know. I finally see. It doesn't matter that the sun is pouring through the open windows: I'm in Darkness.

"Zylynn." Charita moves toward me with her arms out like she's going to hug me and rock me and twist me again, but she can't. I'm finally cured.

I jump to my feet. "*You* are the Liars," I yell. "You are the ones who took me away from the Light. You kidnapped me! And if you don't take me back, I'll never ever please God. You are the evil ones. You are the Liars."

Then I pound up the stairs to wait between the pink stripes for morning.

Except I think and I think when I am in the room and come up with a plan. I can't just follow my map and run away tomorrow. Louis and Charita would find me right away. They have a car so they can go so much faster. They're bigger than me so they can pick me up or tie me down or lock me away until after sunset, until it's too late. Until I'm doomed.

I have to do something to trick them.

I sneak out one last time once everyone is asleep and I am craving pomegranate tea.

I take my flashlight from under my bed where I stored it next to the leftover food from the dinner that they left outside my door. I tiptoe down the stairs.

I sit in the kitchen and pull the folded-up piece of paper out of my pocket.

I pick the phone up from the wall and punch in the numbers.

It rings twice before the familiar bubbly voice answers. "Hello?"

"Jaycia?" I whisper.

"Oh my God," she says. "Zylynn?"

I nod, which is dumb. I've never spoken to a phone before but I know how they work. I know she can't see me.

"Are you OK?" She asks, talking so quickly like she does

now. "It's the middle of the night. Thank God my mom forgot to take my phone after dinner so I have it here. Why are you calling so late? Are you OK?"

"I'm OK," I say. I lie. Again.

Maybe a trick isn't a lie. Maybe it's OK to lie to Liars. And Jaycia is a Liar now too, anyway.

"I can't believe you called," Jaycia is saying. "I was worried I'd never hear from you again. Like, that you'd lose my number or something."

"I didn't," I say.

"Why are you calling so late?" she asks again.

Here we go. Here's the trick.

"I just . . . I needed to talk to someone who . . . would understand . . ."

"Yeah?" Jaycia prompts. "Understand what?"

"I had this big fight with Louis and Charita. I told them I wanted to go home for my ceremony tomorrow and Louis . . . he said . . . I'll never get to go back . . . ever. . . ."

I know I'm about to lie, but the tears are coming from a true place.

"Oh, Zylynn," Jaycia said. "I'm sorry. But of course you can't go back."

"I know," I say. "I get it now."

"You do?" she asks.

"Yeah," I say. "They were lying to us. Inside. Father. He was lying to us."

I'm sorry. I'm sorry. I'm sorry, I tell Father in my head. I hope he understands I'm doing this for him.

"And the Hungry Days. They weren't good," I'm saying. "Kids are supposed to have food."

I'm crying so hard I don't think she'll understand my words, but she does.

"We are, Zylynn. We're supposed to have food. And regular school. And parents."

Jaycia is crying too. Lying makes you cry. And she's a Liar.

"It wasn't fair what they did to me, to us," I say.

It was fair, Father. It was Light and perfect. I'm lying to get back to you.

"It was awful," Jaycia says.

"I'm never going back. I don't want to go back. I want to forget every awful thing that happened to me Inside."

I want to forget every awful thing that happened Outside, in Darkness.

"I never want to see that place again."

I want to be there now.

"I'm so happy, Zylynn," Jaycia is saying. "Oh my God, I'm so happy. I knew you'd figure it out. And every day will be a little easier now. You'll get used to it out here, OK? I promise."

Now, for the second part of my trick.

"There are so many things I want to do," I say. "I want to go back to Target and see the whole thing, every toy and every piece of clothing between the walls. I want to go back to the restaurant and drink all the kinds of sodas and order all kinds of food I've never had before."

"Yes!" Jaycia squeals. "We can do that stuff."

"I want to learn to ride a bike," I say. "I want to play new games on the tablet. Run through a sprinkler."

"I'll teach you," Jaycia says. "I'll teach you to ride a bike! You can practice on mine."

"I want to eat birthday cake and swing on a swing set."

"We can go to the park!" Jaycia says. "We can go so many places. The mall. The library. Maybe we can ride a roller coaster. We can bake cookies. We can learn how to cook so we'll never be hungry again."

The problem is that the dark has twisted me so much that I actually do want to do all of these things. But I won't want that for long. Once I'm Inside, I'll forget all about it.

"Can we start soon?" I ask. "Tomorrow?"

"Yes!" Jaycia squeals. "Can you come over in the morning? I'll give you my address and maybe your dad or stepmom can drive you over?"

"Yeah," I say. "I can get there somehow."

"OK," she says. "My address is Thirty-Eight Oakton Drive. It's right by the little restaurant where we saw you guys."

"Oh wow," I say, my face burning because I'm back to lying. "I can even walk there from here."

"Cool," Jaycia says. "What do you want to do first?"

"Go back to Target," I say. "Or the restaurant. Or find a swing set." I list a bunch of things to confuse her. The more confused she is, the better. Then I say, "Can I bring my sister, Elsie, with me? She'll want to spend my birthday with me too."

I'm getting too used to all the tricking. I don't even flinch when I say *my*.

"Of course!" Jaycia says. "I forgot it was your birthday. We're going to have the best day, I promise. You won't even think about your ceremony."

When she says that I start shaking. I think I've done enough. It's time to hang up.

"Thanks, Jaycia," I say.

"Call me Janice!" she yelps.

I can't stop shaking. I can't stop thinking about all the things she was going to do with me to keep me here until I turned thirteen and was doomed. I can't stop my brain from wondering about a roller coaster or a bicycle or the taste of freshly made cookies.

"OK," I say. Then I hang up.

I go down to the tablet and pull up a new map, this one showing the way to Jaycia's new house. That's what they'll see if they open the tablet in the morning. That's where they'll think I am.

I can get back Inside without them ever finding me.

I've tricked the Liars.

Nineteen

THE FIRST WOBBLY OFF-WHITE BEAM OF the rising sun streaks across my bed and pokes me in the eyes. I'm awake, up, out of the bed and almost smiling in seconds. I pull on my whites. The new ones, from Target. But still white.

Today is the day. I'm thirteen. I go home.

This time I don't try to sneak remnants of Darkness with me into the Light. I pack only what we'll need in Elsie's stolen backpack: extra pairs of socks and underwear, a bar of soap, flashlight, map, Louis's digital watch. No Turtle. No green flip-flops. No Tupperware or plastic bag from under my bed. The bed.

I tiptoe across the hall and open the door to the room with one bed and stuffed animals and coloring books.

"Elsie!" I whisper.

I can see her in the bed, curled on her side so that her face is toward me. It looks almost gold in the slices of sunlight that are sneaking around her curtains. The rest of her room is dark.

Totally dark.

How does she sleep like this?

"Elsie!" I whisper again.

She sits and rubs her eyes. "Zylynn?" she says, too loudly.

I flip the light switch next the door so it's not so dark in there and rush across her carpet. "Shh! Shh!" I say. "You can't wake anyone up!"

"Why?" she asks. She's sitting up in the bed now, but her hands are in front of her eyes like she's trying to hold the Darkness in.

I have to get her out of here.

"We're going to my ceremony, remember? You said you wanted to come."

"Oh yeah!" Elsie says, too loudly again. "Happy birthday!"

"Shh!" I say. I put my hand over her mouth. "You have to whisper, OK?"

She nods. Her head is just a collection of hands going up and down with her two palms over her eyes and mine over her mouth. I take mine away.

"Are you ready?" I say. "Just put on shorts and sneakers. I have everything else you need."

But Elsie lies back down. "I'm tired. Let's go later, OK, Zylynn?"

"No, no!" I whisper. "We have to go now."

I need her to come with me. I need something to offer Father so that he doesn't punish me for a long long time once I turn on the lights.

"Why?" Elsie asks through a yawn.

"Come on," I say, pulling the sheet from her shoulders. "We have to go. We have a long way to walk."

"How long?" Elsie asks.

And then, stupidly, I answer her. "Twelve hours."

"Twelve hours!" she shouts. I reach for her face again but then she whispers, "I know, I know. Be quiet. I'm sorry."

"Come on!" I say.

"I can't walk twelve hours, Zylynn. Let's just wait until Mommy wakes up. She'll drive us."

I stare at the clock next to her head. Minutes tick by. The sun is barely up but I know those minutes are ticking close to sunset.

I reach through my brain, through all of the words I've learned. I search and search for the perfect words to say to make her get up.

But I haven't even started training.

I don't know how to Gather Souls.

Another minute later, I give up. I have to or I'll miss my chance to get home. I'm going to have to deal with the worst punishment Inside. Anything is better than being doomed to Darkness.

Elsie's breathing deeply again. She fell asleep with me sitting right here on the bed.

Father would forgive me so fast if I managed to save a new soul. Father would welcome me back if Elsie was at my side. There would be no Hungry Day, no pinging for the cheese or any of the Abominations and Mistakes I've made in Darkness.

But I can't wait for her. If I'm late getting back, I'm stuck in the Darkness forever. Even the worst pinging or the longest Hungry Day would be better than being doomed.

I watch Elsie sigh in her sleep and shift on her side. I look at her freckles. I think about her making me laugh.

At first I wanted to take Elsie with me just so I would finally be forgiven. But now I can't stand the thought of her sleeping here covered in Darkness, of her being so far from safety, of her turning into another Liar. Like Jaycia.

I lean over and pat her head. "I'll be back for you, Elsie. I'll save you soon."

I tiptoe down the stairs to steal the food I'll need. It's hard to guess exactly how much I should eat in the twelve hours I'll be walking but I know what to take. Only what belongs to me. Only what Father Prophet gave me. Only what's leftover.

I'm listing the items in my head as I reach the bottom of the stairs. The fridge will be my last stop. Fridge, twelve hours of walking, home.

I've been here for so many more than twelve hours. I can wait that long.

I'm so far into my skull, so careful to see nothing but the list of food forming in front of me, I almost miss it. When I look from the kitchen tiles toward the fridge, I lose all my breath.

I'm sure they've finally killed me. Death by a HAPPY

BIRTHDAY ZYLYNN banner and five packages wrapped in winter-sun yellow paper. My heart is choking me.

I pull my eyes away. They were still lying last night. About some things, if not the birthday stuff. If they weren't Liars, they would have taken me home for my ceremony after they promised me I could do whatever I want.

I wind my fingers around the handle of the fridge door and yank. It opens with a whoosh. Cold air rushes at my face. The layers and layers, the shelves upon shelves of food sway in front of my eyes. I've never seen so much. I've never opened a fridge.

Why do they have more than we do? Why is the Darkness less hungry and more comfortable than the Light? We're right and they're wrong. Everything is backward.

I let the list form in front of my eyes again, pushing away the questions. I move around cartons of juice and milk, I lift bags of lunch meat, and shove aside cups of yogurt; I do my best to ignore all of the food at my fingers and only grab what's mine, what was given to me. The tomato I find in one drawer. A bag of grated yellow cheese rests under the lunch meat: close enough. There's a pile of oranges at the top of the fridge. I take one. I squat, looking for the last thing.

Then, there, on the bottom shelf, is my cake. Light pink icing. Hot-pink script on top.

Happy Birthday, Zylynn!
And Welcome Home!

I blink and blink and blink until there's no salt left in my eyes. I stick a finger into the pink and pull back a glop of it to put on my tongue. When the sugar dances there, I have to blink and blink and blink again.

They really were going to give me a cake and presents. They really were telling the truth.

But they're still Liars. Just because they didn't lie about everything doesn't mean they aren't Liars.

I can't think about the ways they were good. I can't wonder if Charita liked me or if Louis was right about them feeding me and treating me well. It's too dangerous to think those things.

Help me get out of here, Father.

I slam the fridge closed. I find a small chocolate bar in the cabinet next to it. I add two water bottles to the backpack and strap it on my back. One more step. One more lie, one more trick to fool the Liars. I pull down the notepad that Charita keeps fastened to the fridge and write on the front sheet.

I went to Jaycia's. It's where I wanted to go since it's my birthday. She told me about a lot of fun stuff we can do out here. We have a lot of exciting plans. I have a map so I know where to go. I'll be back later.

Zylynn

Then I march through the living room determined to get right out the door and never look back.

But there he is. On the couch, curled into the same position I was in yesterday afternoon. Turtle.

I freeze, sad suddenly.

Guilty because I shouldn't be sad.

Angry because they never should have taken me.

I drop Elsie's bag on the wooden floor and pull Turtle from the couch. I squeeze him to my chest. *Good-bye.*

For the last time ever, I tiptoe up the carpeted stairs. I lean over and put him on the floor. I make sure he's sitting up. I make sure it looks like he's waving. I leave him right outside the door where Elsie sleeps.

"Keep her safe from the Darkness until I get back, OK, Turtle?" I whisper.

Then I'm gone.

I stop at the end of the driveway. The sun is barely peeking out from the roof of the house across the street. The sky burns white with only the slightest hint of blue. The air is cool on my bare arms and legs.

I glance at Louis's watch: 5:27.

I take a deep breath. The cool air goes from my lungs into my legs and arms and tummy and brain. It tastes good. It tastes like home.

The backpack is light and warm, only a whisper on my shoulders. I feel Father Prophet's hand resting on my head. I close my eyes, concentrate, and then, in front of me, I see it. Finally. His whole face.

It's a sign.

If I can walk straight through I'll be there by 5:27 p.m. Way before sunset.

I take a step into the road. I'm on my way.

Twenty

I had just swallowed my last gulp of tea when the screen door of the Girls' Dorm bounced open.

"Zylynn!" The deep voice of Brother Wrinkesley boomed.

All of our heads were immediately off the pillows, startled. After bedtime, the only noises were nightmares. Or worse.

"Zylynn! Get out here," he said.

This was the worst. Worse than a nightmare. This was a punishment. A punishment after bedtime could only mean one thing.

All of the girls looked at me. They knew where I was going.

I felt tiny. I felt dirty.

I dug my fingers into my feather mattress, trying to make it suck me in. I knew. If I left this dorm, I would be like Jaycia and the others who were yanked away. I would not see anything for a long time. Or, like her, forever.

I also snuck out and ate cheese. I also stayed up while she laughed. I let her tell me all about balloons and bicycles. I stole food and ate on a Hungry Day. I was evil and dirty and wrong. And now I was being punished. Cast out.

"Zylynn." His voice bounced off all the beds and landed on my pillow. "Now!"

I slipped out of the bed. I skated across the sandy floor. Brother Wrinkesley was biting his lips. He didn't look as scary as he sounded. But there was another man with him, dressed in almost all black: pants, shoes, jacket, tie. He carried a shiny black box that dangled from a silver handle.

He looked like one of the strangers who sometimes showed up in Chapel or School or the Dining Hall.

He tried to put his hand on my shoulder but I ran. Not far. Only five feet or so from where they were standing. Only so far that I knew the stranger wasn't going to touch me.

"It's time," Brother Wrinkesley said. "You have to go now."

"I don't want to!" I said. I knew they'd hear me in the dorms. I knew they'd wonder what made me so evil and dirty. I knew they'd be sad for me but more relieved for themselves, secretly listing all of the Mistakes they'd made; secretly wondering why it was me and not them.

The stranger tried to touch me again. Brother Wrinkesley called, "Back off," and then suddenly Brother Chansayzar and Brother Wrinkesley were holding my elbows before I even saw them. They lifted me by the armpits. They walked me straight through the first circle until we reached the hedges and the walls and the dogs and I thought *no, no, no, no, no don't go through there I can't go through there it's Darkness through there.*

Brother Chansayzar whispered to me the whole time. "You'll be OK, you'll be OK."

Brother Wrinkesley rubbed my shoulder with the hand that wasn't holding me.

The walls got closer and closer and closer until I saw, just in front of the dogs, ten or twenty feet away. There he was. Father Prophet.

I squinted to be sure, but he was there. I felt myself relax in the men's arms. Father would not let them take me. He knew that even when I made Mistakes, I was trying. We can't be perfect; he said so all the time. Only Father Prophet could be perfect. He would understand. He would protect us.

He would not let the Darkness suck me up.

And then we were past him. And then we were Outside. And then they dropped me on the Darkness dirt. And then life was over.

Father Prophet didn't even wave.

That's how evil I am.

Twenty-One

I'VE BEEN WALKING FOR AN HOUR. I'm already on the second street. Only four streets to go, which makes it seem like it can't take another eleven hours, but I can see from the map that the third street is a long one.

ZOOM!

I leap away from the speeding car, into the grass. A dog comes sprinting at me, barking so loudly I dive into a row of bushes at the house next door.

My heart is beating so hard against my collarbone it vibrates.

I should have thought of these things before: cars, dogs, other people. I'll have to work to stay invisible.

I can't be afraid of these things.

I can't wish for Charita or Louis.

I have to keep walking.

I have to get home.

It's 8:17.

I know now why there is so much sunshine in Darkness.

Mother God is Light but Mother God is not the sun. The sun is evil.

It beats on my head, baking my hair into the skin of my skull. Sweat stings my forehead and eyes and tickles between my shoulder blades. The sun turns the backpack into a hot stone rubbing my white shirt back and forth, back and forth until the skin beneath it is raw and sore.

I'm sort of used to the cars rushing past. I only jump when it's a loud one. I don't know why they have to go that fast.

I don't know why there are so many cars or so many people who stay here in the Darkness or how these people are suffering.

But I know that they're suffering. That's what I learned. The Darkness means suffering.

I make my third turn onto the long road. Keep taking step after step after step.

After step.

This is all for you, Father. I'm coming home.

The sun climbs higher.

Step.

After step.

After step.

It's 9:24. I drain the last of my first bottle of water on to my cracked tongue. My skin absorbs it before I can even swallow.

Something I never knew before: a Thirsty Day is worse than a Hungry Day.

I'm only eight hours away and I'm already on the long road. I decide I get a break. I sit on the curb and watch the cars fly by my toes. I know now that they won't hit me.

No one looks at the girl on the road. My light is so bright they can't even see me.

Step.

After step.

After hot step.

I'm still on the third road. It's 10:11 and it's still 10:11 and it's still 10:11. Every time I check Louis's watch it says the same thing over and over and over until it finally moves only one digit. No wonder they check their watches constantly in Darkness.

Louis and Charita were always looking at their watches as if they didn't know where to be. But maybe it's because they didn't have to be only one place. In the Darkness there are choices. Even this is sort of a choice. I chose to go home.

I'm choosing my ceremony.

I'm choosing my ceremony over cake and ice cream and presents.

It makes me a little dizzy. Choices seem good but they're scary. Because if you don't have a choice, you can't choose wrong.

But I'm not choosing wrong. I'm choosing the Light.

The third road coils endlessly in front of me, twisting,

dipping out of sight, rising up again until it meets the hazy sun at the end of the sky.

The sun assaults my skin, my sweat, my eyes. I take another sip of water. I have only three sips left, but the third road has to end soon.

Another step.

I take my backpack off and carry it by the strap.

Another step.

My back is happy to breathe.

Another step.

But my shoulder is being yanked from its socket.

It's exactly noon when I see him. My legs have slowed, my sneakers scraping the sidewalk to move my feet forward. My shoulders droop. My wrist comes toward my eyes over and over and over again every minute but time rarely inches forward. The backpack hangs from my right hand or my left hand or a shoulder or my neck, constantly moving but never comfortable. My T-shirt sticks to my skin, my shorts rub against the inside of my legs.

I'm out of water.

I think I'll die. I'll die in Darkness.

But then I see him. He's on the long road, just in front of me, his white cape dazzling behind him, his gray eyes huge and focused on me, his arms outstretched. I only have to reach him.

He finally came to get me. I'm finally good enough.

I pick up a foot. I really move forward. Five steps. Ten. Twenty. Fifty. Sixty-seven.

Poof! He disappears.

I freeze, confused. The cars rush past the sweaty blond girl. They don't see me. Neither did Father.

Then I look to my left and I almost sing for joy. This is where he led me. He's saving my life so I can get home and save my Light.

I know what it is.

> **Park** (n.): an area of land, usually in a largely natural state, for the enjoyment of the public, having facilities for rest and recreation, often owned, set apart, and managed by a city, state, or nation

There're picnic tables for sitting and big, leafy trees from which glorious shade spreads out onto the grass. And, most importantly, there's a concrete structure right at the front.

> **Water fountain** (n.): a public fountain to provide a jet of drinking water

I run at it. I step onto the concrete square at the base, lean over it, and hit the metal button with my knee. A hard stream of water slaps me in the lips and I suck it down, into my system, until it fills my stomach and my lungs and my body all the way to my fingers and toes. Then I fill up both water bottles and walk to the base of a tree.

I pull my knees to my chest, making sure there's no part of the sun hitting any of my skin.

Lunchtime.

No, not lunchtime. Lunch is for the Outside. Just eating time.

I pull out the tomato and the cheese. I take a huge bite of the red fruit and a stream of juice and seeds runs down my water-fountain-wet chin. I use my fingers to push as much of the tomato guts back into my mouth as possible. I suck on my fingers until they are more spit-y than tomatoey. I don't want to waste a single bit. I take a sip of my water. Then I squeeze my thumb and forefinger into the cheese, pull out a few strips, and chew.

I breathe, I suck in the shade.

More water. More tomato. More cheese. More shade.

I sit like that—eating, drinking, breathing—until I feel that pinch in my cheek. I'm smiling.

I cannot be smiling. I cannot be happy.

I'm still in Darkness.

I shove the rest of the tomato in my mouth, chew, swallow.

Even though it feels like the cars can't see me, I sneak behind the tree to pull my shorts down, squat, and pee. I go back to the water fountain to fill up my bottles.

When I look back at the long road, I realize that if I walk across the people's grass, I'll get more time to walk under their trees and in the shade.

It should be easier now with a full stomach and two fresh bottles of water. I shouldn't need another break.

Twenty-Two

STEP.

Step.

Step.

Step.

The sun beats, pounds, squishes my head.

Step.

As the shadows of houses and trees spread farther and farther into the street, my feet get heavier and heavier until it feels like my sneakers are made of the same stone as the Chapel benches. My calves and knees and thighs shake. I move forward, my sneakers scraping the road, Elsie's backpack trailing behind me, dragged by only my index finger.

The bag gets lighter and my head gets heavier as my water supply dwindles.

Please save me. Please don't let me die this close to home, this close to turning on the lights in the Chapel.

And then I see the next step. Still yards and miles away, but clearly there. The end of the third road: the shrugging cactus. I'm more than halfway through my journey.

I think I'm about a half hour behind, but that's OK. Even if I get there two hours late, I'll still beat the sunset.

And rising up on the corner, like a thirteen-year-old girl with her arms over her head at the front of the Chapel, is a water fountain. I pick up my feet. I ignore the pain and the sun and the sweat and the cars silver and tan and green, big and small and boxy. Everything around my laser vision turns flimsy and fake. I see only the water fountain. By the time I reach it, the world is swinging dangerously beneath my eyes and I'm almost running. I get there just as I think I might fall, reaching out both arms and hugging the concrete mini-tower like I am Charita and it is Jakey. I take a long sip, then dunk my entire head under the stream, then sip again.

I fill up my bottles and sneak to the shade behind the concrete structure to sip on the water and eat some cheese. Slowly, my heart lowers itself to the proper spot behind my chest bone, my sweat stops flowing and sticks to my skin, my vision slows back to normal.

I notice that I'm sitting on a patch of muddy red clay. Red clay. Like home.

I'm almost there, Father. Almost. I remember you.

I lean my head back against the concrete to shut my eyes and let his face form on my eyelids.

Twenty-Three

BEEP! BEEP! BEEP!

My eyes spring open.

Beep! Beep! Beep!

Louis's watch is making the worst sound over and over and over.

Beep! Beep! Beep!

I don't know how to stop it. It keeps going and going and I cower behind the water fountain cradling my wrist.

Beep! Beep! Beep!

Finally, I pound it against the concrete behind me and it stops the noises. I check it to be sure the seconds are still ticking.

5:22:37

5:22:38

5:22:39

Wait . . . 5:22. No. That can't be. I've only been sitting here a minute.

I jump to my feet and they scream back at me. I look up and the bones in my neck go *crack-crack-crack-crack*. Yes, the sun has started its slow sinking toward the earth. The shadows are stretching to meet the other side of the road. It's late afternoon somehow: I have to be there by evening or I'll be banished from the light forever.

For the first time it occurs to me that I might not make it. I might be alive at the end of this, but I might be late.

I put one foot in front of me. My legs feel even more stiff after that rest, like I'm made of fabric that's stitched too tight. But I force my knees to bend, my feet to move, my body to turn down the fourth road.

I have to keep moving. I have to be there by evening.

5:33

5:57

6:09

6:18

I'm not used to time. We don't pay much attention to it Inside. But I thought every minute was the same. I'm not sure if I was taught that, or if I assumed it. But, I think, Inside every minute is the same.

Out here, time crawls when I want it to move and rushes when I need it to stop.

Father, please give me enough time to see you. I know it's my fault. I should've run away as soon as I got there. I know I'm guilty and I'm dirty and evil now, but please. I want to be in the

Light. Give me enough time to get back.

But Father Prophet doesn't answer. He still doesn't answer. He's disappeared from me as surely as I've disappeared from the compound. He said we'd only have to want to come back. He said we'd only have to remember. After days and days of trying and trying to remember he's still gone. He . . .

I can't stop my prayer from tumbling forward, tossing itself into places it's not supposed to go.

Mother God, you are the master of everything and time is a part of everything. Please slow it down because I need to get to your Light. I need to be a part of it forever. I can't rot in Darkness. I need to stand in your Chapel and turn on your lights before the sun sets today. It's my birthday. Thirteen, Mother. I have to.

I shouldn't be praying to her. Father wouldn't want me to. But I think this is an emergency.

If I don't make it by sunset . . . Louis and Charita won't want me back. They'll be mad I ran away and tricked them. They won't give me clothes and food and a bed anymore.

If I don't make it by sunset . . . I will have nowhere left to go.

6:34

I turn onto the final road. It's a long one that twists and turns right into the huge ball of a sun. The sun won't listen to me. It keeps sliding down the sky no matter how much I beg it not to.

I make my legs keep moving. I've only seen Inside from the Outside once before, but I remember so my eyes keep squinting for the whitewashed walls of my compound, my safe place, my home.

Step.

Step.

Step.

6:48

I take the orange out of my bag. I still see nothing.

Peel. Step.

Peel. Step.

Bite. Step.

7:02

This road has no end. The sunbeams slice the earth. The skin on my face is so hot it's trying to slip off my bones.

The map might be a lie. I can't believe I didn't think of that before. The map came from Darkness. It might be a lie.

It's time. I give up.

I'll drop into the middle of the road and let the green boxy car that's approaching decide what to do with me: a sweaty, hungry, tired, broken girl lost in Darkness. It can run me over. It can torture me. There's nothing left for me to decide.

If the map was a lie, my Light is out. Forever.

All I've wanted was Father. All I've asked for is to go home.

What I've gotten is Louis and Charita. And Junior and Elsie and Jakey. I know that they're Outsiders and Liars. I'm not supposed to trust anything they say. I'm not supposed to give them any of my words. But the past ten days have been the hardest of my life. I've begged and begged and begged Father Prophet for help, but it almost feels like the Liars care about me more than he does.

Why haven't you helped me, Father? Where are you?

But then—and it's only a speck in my vision—there's a square of white on the horizon. In front of it, a see-through version of the young Father Prophet waves his hand and urges me along. So I stay on the side of the road. I take another shaky step. Then another, then another, until that green car is in front of me, showing me that I'm still invisible and this isn't over yet. Young Father poofs back into invisibility too.

I can see it. The whitewashed walls announcing the front of the compound. The path leading in is the same red mud that I usually have between my toes. The roofs peeking over the walls are silver and glint-y and exactly what I should be seeing every time I look up to the sky. The Chapel tower stands tall and proud and stone in the middle. The light from the sun's lowest beam rests just on top of it, like Mother God is balancing on the tower on her tippy-toes, looking for me, waiting for me.

"I'm coming," I whisper, even though I know I shouldn't talk to her. It's no longer an emergency.

I dash behind the nearest bush to get myself ready. I peel off my shorts and shirt, ring out the sweat and change my socks and underwear. I pour some water on my head and smooth my hair back. I won't have a pretty dress and a head full of sparkling pins for my ceremony, but at least I'll be sort of clean.

Then I ditch Elsie's backpack. I ditch Elsie herself, and Junior and Jakey. I ditch Louis and Uncle Alan and strawberries and colors and ice cream. I ditch Target and Turtle and Charita. I ditch Darkness right there on the side of the road.

And I run toward the Light.

Twenty-Four

AS THE COMPOUND COMES SPEEDING IN front of me, I slow to a walk, then a tiptoe.

I made it. *Thank you, thank you. I made it.*

I wonder why Father Prophet and the Teachers and Caretakers never told us what it looked like from the Outside: how the walls are the same pristine white above the prickly hedges that hug them inside and out; how they stretch so high they could scratch the bottom of the clouds if there were any; how from the Outside our home looks like nothing but walls and shining silver roofs.

I wonder why they never told us anything real about the Outside. I wonder why they only gave us words and no information. The words were not enough. Why didn't they give us a map? Or chains to pull ourselves back with? I had to grow my own chains to get back here.

But I don't want to think about that now. I don't want to think about all of the times it felt like Father let me down. Or how, sometimes, it seemed like the Liars took better care of me than the Light. I'll push all of that from my mind until I forget.

I'm back now. I'm back.

I can see only one break in the wall that snakes across the end of the road. It's a wooden gate slumping in the middle of all of that white concrete. I see it and then I see everything from ten days ago and then I'm shaking. But those gates, they're parted slightly, and I know that they're left open for me and that this nightmare-that-was-real is almost over. I stand still in front of them and listen. The entire wall, the entire compound, is breathing, snoring. I can hear the in and out, in and out, in and out. It begs me to slip inside and turn on the Chapel lights and wake it up.

I tiptoe tiptoe tiptoe until I could reach out a hand and touch the weathered splinters of the Darkness side of the gate. It is the last bit of Darkness that I will ever touch.

Then I jump.

The dogs erupt into ferocious barking and scamper around where they're tied to both sides of the wall. I can hear them all, even the ones I can't see. The ones I can see strain against their chains and jump at me with claw-filled paws batting in front of their faces and they waggle their heads quick quick quick showing off every shiny, pointy, gray tooth.

I don't run.

I forgot about the dogs. Worse: they forgot about me. What if everyone did?

When the noise they're making goes unanswered—no alarmed screaming from the kids Inside, none of the men appearing out of breath to make sure that the Light is safe from a Dark infiltrator—I know the day is over in there. They're all already asleep. I look at the sky. The sun is low, but there. I still have time.

I didn't come this far to give up only because it's after teatime.

I'll have to wake up Father Prophet.

I know how to calm the dogs down. They taught us over and over again every day or every week or something how to stay safe if the dogs ever forget us. "Shh, shh," I say. I sit on the ground. "I'm here for the Light," I say.

They get quieter. Some of them hide their teeth behind their gums.

"Shh, shh." I crawl toward the gate and—"Shh, shh"—crack it open with my palm. "I'm here for the Light." But that last sentence is just for me. The dogs are lying still again. They remember me now.

Then I'm Inside. Home.

Even the darkening air smells like her Light.

I tiptoe down the main path until I stand right at the entrance to the first, the smallest circle of buildings: Girls' Dorm to my left, Dining Hall on my right, bathroom, Boys' Dorm, and classrooms spread out across the empty circle. This circle is small enough to see all of the buildings, even the ones across from where I stand. It's like I remember. Everything, except the emptiness, is the same. My breath tastes like music: I made it. My heart becomes one of those helium balloons Jaycia told me about, so big and light and high in my body I'm sure I'll float away straight to Mother God herself: I'm thirteen.

Tonight, my ceremony. Tomorrow, I start training to Gather.

Before I take another step, I crouch and slip off my shoes and socks. Whoever heard of a Thirteenth Ceremony while wearing shoes? I smile to myself, the picture is so funny.

I tiptoe about ten paces to the right, then pull open the screen door to the Girls' Dorm. I'll stash my shoes and socks—I'll need them for Exercise tomorrow—then I'll run across the compound to fetch Father.

He might want to wake everyone up for my ceremony anyway. Or else it'll be just him and me. I don't know which one I want more.

Light. That's all I want.

The door creaks when it opens and I gasp, sure I'm about to be caught. Who is in charge now? Sunuko? Or Lixathia?

No one moves. The only noises are sighs and shifting sheets. (And folding stomachs: it was a Hungry Day. I can tell by the sound of it.) I step from the clay path to the sandy floor and let the door bounce shut behind me. A wall of pomegranate tea slaps me in the nostrils. Did it always smell this strong?

Still, no one stirs.

I drop each shoe onto the floorboards with a thud.

Then my heart stops. Why am I doing this? What if they

don't even remember me? What if they hate me now?

There are visions folded into the dark and twisted parts of my brain: hugs and cheering and "happy birthdays" but I know those things are impossible here. I didn't ever want the impossible until Louis stole my Light.

A beam of sunshine comes through the window and pokes me in the eye, like it did this morning. Waking up feels like days and weeks and months ago now.

These sleeping girls won't sing at my Ceremony but that's OK because I will. I will sing. I will turn on the lights. I made it.

The red dust that collects on the soles of my feet feels as good as a hug as I scurry through the second circle. I pass two classrooms and the Exercise Fields and the Teen Dorms, and then, at the very center of everything, the Chapel.

I can't help but slow down and glance inside the cracked-open metal doors. The stone benches look gray and shadowy from out here even though I know they're white. The windows are high and I can see the light still falling through the one closest to the door. But I don't have much time.

Do I go in now? Do I try to do it once without Father? Do I make sure I have the Light, first?

No. I'm here. I did more to get here by thirteen than any other girl has done ever. I went through so much to turn those lights on. She has to be pleased with me. It will work.

If I get back to the Chapel with Father in time.

I run through the rest of the second circle.

I know where Father Prophet lives even though I've never been there. In fact, I've barely ever been in the third circle: the last time I remember crossing from second to third was a year ago to see Brother Tomlinkin. The third circle is the most exciting and interesting, so full of paths and buildings and fields that you can't even see that it's shaped like a circle unless you walk all the way around it. I don't know what most of the buildings are for. Before, I never wondered. Today, I don't have time. I rush past big ones and small ones to the very back end of those whitewashed walls. To Father Prophet's house.

I climb up the front stairs slowly. They're made of stone, like the Chapel. Nothing else here is made of stone, but these stairs are. In fact, his whole house is. I reach out a hand and touch my knuckles to the wall to be sure. Yes: stone.

Why is it stone when the rest of us sleep in plywood and metal? Why does Father have his own house and the rest of us have dorms? Why have I never thought of this before?

And why is there noise, so much noise, spilling out of the windows over my head when the rest of the compound is empty and asleep?

I knock. I knock and knock and knock but he doesn't come.

It's too noisy. He can't hear me.

But he should already know I'm here. I've been talking to him all day.

I wait a second, check the setting sun, then knock again. His door is different too: big and metal and heavy like Louis and Charita's door.

No one comes.

I reach for the knob, my fingertips sizzling on the hot metal surface. It turns. Then I'm inside.

"Good night, sweet Zylynn," a deep voice said.

My tiny body was wrapped tight in blankets and tucked next to another snoring body. A woman's body.

There was a man leaning over us.

"I'll miss you," he said.

I strained to open my eyes, to move my arms out of the blankets, to shake my head, to get my thick, pomegranate-coated tongue to speak. To do anything to make that voice stay another minute.

I was so . . . so . . . tired . . .

Lips brushed against the top of my head.

"Your momma's gonna take good care of you, Zy-baby. I know she will. And this isn't good-bye. It's just . . . see you later. I've got to . . . figure some things out, but—"

Why wouldn't my eyes open? Why couldn't I move my mouth to tell him to stay?

"I'll be back," he finished.

I heard him turn. I heard footsteps getting further from the bed.

I finally pried my left eye open. Just in time to see him disappear through the screen door.

Daddy.

Louis.

Twenty-Five

THE HALLWAY IS DARK. SO DARK. I didn't know dark like this existed in Light, Inside, in Father's house. The floor is made of wood but not like our floor in the dorm. It's fancy, polished, deep brown wood.

Above my head there's nothing but noise: calling and shouting, music from some sort of music-player, laughing, singing, chairs scraping, feet bouncing off the floor, and the clinking of utensils against plates.

There are many voices. More than just Father's. But his is there, clear, distinct, low, powerful. He's right above my head.

In front of me there's a set of carpeted stairs.

Carpet. Music. Shouting.

Curiosity is wound around me so tightly now I can't make myself move. She squeezes my legs and stomach and arms and shoulders. She pushes frigid fingers into each muscle and freezes them one by one. She whispers two storms of questions, one into each ear, making them meet in the middle of my skull and morph and multiply until I'm no longer made of blood and organs but only words and questions.

I don't know how long it takes me to move, but I know the sun is still there. Here. Outside this dark house, in the sky.

Curiosity is still here too, a backpack filled with bricks rubbing against the raw skin on my shoulders and back. But I manage to contain her so that I can move.

Father's carpet is not soft on the soles of my feet. It's scratchy. Softness is for the Outside. Light has edges.

I count the steps: One, two, three, four . . . and then, twelve. I'm at the top. There's a small hallway and at the end is a bright room crammed with noise. Curiosity hangs like a chain on one foot, fear on the other, as I take three steps to get to the doorway of the room.

I shouldn't be afraid anymore. I'm back Inside. I'm finding Father.

But fear hangs from me anyway, heavy and smelly and there.

I gape in the open doorway. I think I might actually be invisible because I stand there for seconds or minutes or hours and no one notices.

I know what I'm seeing. I know what it is.

> **Party** (n.): a social gathering of invited guests to one's home or elsewhere for purpose of conversation, refreshment, entertainment, etc.

But how can a word from Outside Studies tell me about something that's happening Inside?

There are men and women around a big table. More women, maybe six and only three or four men. I recognize them. Brother Wrinklesky. Brother Chansayzar. Only the most important men are here. The rest must be where they should be: sleeping in the Men's Dorm.

But the women—there are only a few of them here too—they shouldn't be Inside at all. Not yet.

At the end of the table, even larger than I remember him, is Father. He holds up a goblet filled with red liquid and bounces back and forth on his toes singing something I can't understand. Two women hug him on either side and then . . . Father plants his fat lips into their hair. He kisses them.

I almost retch in the doorway. What is this?

Another man, Brother Crissakey—I recognize him as the doctor who took over for Brother Tomlinkin—circles the table with a bottle and adds more red liquid to everyone's glasses. The women all sort of rock where they're sitting or standing. And in front of everyone is a plate heaping with all sorts of things—meat and green vegetables and rice and potatoes and gravy. An entire roasted bird sits in the center of the table.

"But today was a Hungry Day." I say it out loud, but no one can hear me through the music and the sloppy laughter.

Father Prophet spins one of the ladies around in his arms and lets go. She stumbles a few steps toward a little table in the corner. I get distracted by that table for a second because I see a big TV on it. We have television? And next to the TV I see something small and silver and shiny and terrifying. I know what it is. But it can't be that.

I can't help thinking of all the times he stood up in Chapel and talked about the evil, the violence, the guns in Darkness.

> **Gun** (n.): a weapon consisting of a metal tube, with mechanical attachments, from which projectiles are shot by the force of an explosive

> **Gun** (n.): the most obvious sign of evil, greed, and Darkness

How can he have one in his own living room? Has it always been here? Does he carry it around? Has it been in the Chapel?

There are so many things in this room that don't belong Inside, that belong only in Darkness: guns and televisions and wine and hugging and kissing and laughter.

I can't try to understand it. I can't let the questions spinning in my brain take a shape. I can't let Curiosity win.

There's probably only a few minutes until sunset. I have to get to the Chapel with Father.

Once I'm a full part of the Light, once I turn those lights on, once Mother shows him how pleased she is with me, then I will understand. Or I will forget. Either one is better than standing in this doorway shaking with my eyes getting wet and my feet so sore and my head so stuffed with words and questions.

"Zylynn!" a lady gasps.

I'm not invisible after all.

All of the men and women in the room freeze. The singing stops. The music buzzes off. Their eyes swing to find me cowering in the doorway while I turn my head back and forth until I find the smallest, skinniest, most-alone woman huddled under layers of white dress on the window seat in the corner. "Zylynn?" she says again. A question this time.

It's Thesmerelda.

She stands with her arms reaching for me and I know everything that I don't want to know: this is my mother. Not like God, but like Charita said. This is my mother. This is—

"Tessie!" Father's voice booms across the room. "Sit. You know you cannot touch that child."

Thesmerelda sits and so does everyone else. They lock their lips and deaden their eyes. They sit straight and still like they're in Chapel. It's like they all climbed back into their Inside bodies and forgot what was going on only seconds ago.

I can forget too. I can forget that the woman I'm staring at is my mother. I can join the Light and forget everything I've seen. I promise.

I don't know why I'm talking to him in my head with Father right in front of me. I thought he was with me all day, but now he looks surprised to see me.

"Zylynn," Father says. "Come here."

He sits on his chair. It's different from everyone else's: made of stone instead of that dark shiny wood, filled with cushions, bigger and taller, like his throne in the Chapel.

"Come!" he says again. He puts his hand out like he wants me to stand with my head underneath it. I don't know why I'm shaking. I used to stand with his hand on my head or my cheek all the time.

I have to walk past the still and silent men and women to get there. There are women here, and there shouldn't be. But that's not the worst part. I got used to that with Charita. The worst is that they're so still, like they're Elsie's dolls instead of real people.

Then his hand is on my head. I should feel calm. I should feel good. I can't stop Curiosity from ruining this for me.

"Do not be afraid of this, child," Father says. His gray eyes search my face deeply. It's instantly familiar. I relax. "Do not be afraid. You walked into a private feast, that's all. Doesn't this look like a Feast Day to you?"

It does. I nod.

"Well, sometimes I host a small Feast Day for the most important men and women. For the ones who work the hardest. That will be you one day, will it not?"

It will be me. I will work so hard for Father Prophet, for Mother God. It will be me at this private feast.

"It might seem strange to you," Brother Wrinkesley adds from behind me. "But Father says this is how Mother God would want it to be. Mother rewards us for our special commitment and dedication."

Brother Wrinkesley sort of speaks like he's reciting the definition of a word in Outside Studies. But I can tell he believes it too.

"This doesn't happen all the time, these private feasts," Father says. And Brother Crissakey starts laughing. I don't get the joke, but that's OK. I'll understand everything soon. If not, I'll forget it. Father keeps talking. "It must have been strange for you to walk in on this feast since you haven't heard of it yet. But I'm sure that answers your questions, right, child? Now tell me, why are you here?"

But he didn't answer all of my questions. Curiosity floods my brain again. If this is a feast, why do the women look like they're dead? If it's a private feast with all this food, why did all of the girls in the dorm have to have a Hungry Day today? Why is this house so nice with stone and carpet? Why . . .

I'll choose one question. Father doesn't like questions the way Charita does. So I'll choose only one. I point to his table where the gun is. "Why—"

"Shh, child," Father says. "Tell me why you're here. How did you get here? Did Louis finally find enough sense in his heart to return you to where you can be safe forever?"

Thesmerelda's head whips up and her eyes come to life for a second. And I remember. Louis was here. He was Inside. He belonged to Father once too. Like me. Like my new mother who is sitting in the corner.

But Louis had nothing to do with me being here today. I shake my head.

"Did you convince your new family that you had to get back to where you can find Mother God and ultimate salvation?"

My voice is so small. "I wanted my ceremony," I whisper.

"Your ceremony?" Father's eyebrows jump. "You convinced them to take you back here for your Thirteenth Ceremony?"

"I . . . I walked," I say.

"What?" He pauses. "Are you saying they don't know you're here?" Father is speaking quickly now. More quickly than I've ever heard him speak. It's like he starts saying a word before he's finished saying the one before. I have to work to understand him.

"They don't know anything, I promise. I ran away. I walked all day to get here."

"What?" Father says again. He's loud now. Almost like he's scared. Or angry. Maybe angry.

"I wanted my ceremony," I say again. "It's my birthday," I say.

"It's her birthday," Thesmerelda/Tessie says at the same time. I look across the room. Her hair is yellow, like mine. Like Uncle Alan's beard. What would it be like if she hugged me?

I shake my head. No questions. Father said no questions. Not even in my brain. No questions anywhere.

Curiosity: I give you up. I renounce you.

"You think you deserve a ceremony?" Father Prophet is laughing but I don't understand it. "After you spent ten days in Darkness, you think you can march back in here at the last minute and we'll drop everything and throw you a ceremony?"

So we do have laughing here. But it doesn't sound as nice. It doesn't sound nice at all.

"I don't need the whole thing," I say quickly. "I only need to turn the lights on."

He laughs again. It's like each chuckle chops an inch off my legs. Mother God is making me shorter.

"Don't tell me what you need, girl," he says. He grabs both of my shoulders in his fleshy palms and holds too tight. "Don't act like you know the Mother better than I do."

"Father—" There's a voice in the back but he keeps talking.

"You think you're pleasing to the Mother?"

I nod. "I walked all day to get here," I say. "Fourteen hours or more. It was supposed to take twelve but I passed out and then I kept walking and it took fourteen. I walked it all. Just to get here. Just to be a part of the Light forever and I—"

"Well, that was a waste of time." His words bite me in the face. "Don't pretend I don't know every horrible thing you did out there. Don't think I don't know every evil, dirty thing you let them tell you, you let yourself think or do or say or smell or touch or . . . taste."

I'm shaking now but I'm not doing it myself. It's my body shaking between his hands. He's shaking me.

"You were a bad, bad girl," he growls. "You forgot all about your one true Father and Mother."

"No," I say.

Everyone in the room gasps. We aren't allowed to say that word to him.

Still, my brain screams it. *NO!* "I thought of you every day. I prayed every night."

"You believed every lie the Darkness told you."

"No. No. I didn't. I tried not to believe anything."

Father keeps on yelling. "You decided life was all about money and greed and having things."

"No! I didn't think like that." *No one thought like that.*

He's wrong. Father can't be wrong but he is wrong.

"Father," Brother Wrinkesley says. "Don't you think we should explain—"

He doesn't listen. He keeps on yelling.

"You can't go trying to turn on the lights in Mother's Chapel now, Zylynn," he says. He shoves me to the ground. I land on my hands and knees, looking up at him. "She knows you're nothing but a dirty, evil girl. You don't even deserve to be called Zylynn."

Mother God? I ask. I don't even care if I'm bothering her. *Am I dirty? Mother?*

"Stop!" Thesmerelda screams. I hear her feet on the wooden floor behind me and then her fingers are like feathers on my elbows, pulling me up. She spreads her arms but before she can get them all the way around me, Father shoots his hand back like he's about to hit her in the face.

"NO!" I yell.

We all freeze.

Her arms are open. I want to step into them. I want her to hold me close. This is the body that grew me before I could grow myself. This is the woman who was supposed to take care of me when I was hungry and when I was sad and when I was confused. This is my Charita. This is my *mother.*

She didn't do those things. But I want to hug her anyway.

I take a step toward her. Father's arm is frozen in the air like if she hugs me, he'll hit her.

I've never seen Father hit anyone. I've never seen an adult get hit. Usually it's only the Caretakers or the other kids who hit someone. And usually it's only if someone makes a Mistake.

Thesmerelda hasn't made a Mistake.

She takes another step closer to me.

"Don't hug that child," Father says deeply, slowly. "Don't hug that child unless you want to go right where she's going."

She takes a step back. Her feather-fingers are gone. Her eyes look dead again. Everyone's eyes are dead except mine and Father's and his look . . . awful.

He drops his hand.

"Wait downstairs," he commands. "Brother Wrinkesley will come down in a minute and he'll call Louis. He'll have that Agent of Darkness come and get you and take you back where you belong now."

The entire room stares at Father, mouths open, dead eyes slightly less dead.

"Really?" they start to say.

"That's it?"

"Is that really best?"

"Shouldn't you tell her?"

He flicks his eyes off me to yell at them—"Shut up!"—and I run. Out of the room, through the small hallway, down the scratchy stairs, onto the red path, I run and run and run.

I can't turn to look, but somehow I feel Thesmerelda's eyes in the window, watching my escape. I feel her smile.

My feet and legs burn. My lungs are ready to burst and give up. But I run. I run back through the third circle, through half of the second circle. I run until I am at the building, up the stairs and inside the tall, stone doors. There, I bend over and suck in breath.

Her Chapel spreads before me: exactly the same as it is every day when it's stuffed full of all of the Children Inside the Light. But it also looks different. It looks happier, for some reason, all white stone and high windows and the tiny last wisps of sunlight sneaking through them like her fingers. It's weird to be alone in the Chapel but it's also OK. I'm here. I'm alive. I'm me. I know I'm making her happy.

I'm calm.

Once my breath is back in my body, I stand and stretch until my spine is as straight as it will go.

I will not think about Father or Jaycia or Louis or Thesmerelda or any of the people who are not here and should be. I spent thirteen years learning about her, learning about how to become a full member of her Light. I spent fourteen hours or more walking here to do this today. I know exactly what to do.

I will throw my own ceremony.

I open my mouth.

"Oh Mother God . . ."

I almost stop, startled at my voice. It's high and raspy and young and it doesn't match how I feel inside: like I know more than everyone, like I'm even closer to Mother God than Father Prophet, like I'm made entirely of Light.

"Oh Light of all Lights . . ."

I take my first step down the aisle, singing as I go. My imagination fills the benches with all of the people who should be here. Every last drop of sunlight slides warm across my face as I step-sing, step-sing, step-sing down the aisle.

"I am yours."

My bare feet climb the metal rafters at the front of the Chapel and then I'm on the stage where I've never been before. I stand with my back to Father's chair, about five feet in front of it, and I study her Chapel as it is—made of nothing but stone and sunset. It's so beautiful. I wonder how I never noticed that before. I wonder why at every other Thirteenth Ceremony the chapel has been full and I've been empty.

But it will be night soon. I can tell by looking through the high windows, it will be dark in minutes.

Here we go.

I'm not nervous. I have never been less nervous since I left the Inside ten days ago.

Once I turn the lights on, everything will make sense. Father Prophet will know, somehow. She'll tell him. He'll explain everything or I'll just know, or somehow it will make sense why the Darkness has so many good things that we don't have here and why there were women in that room when the women aren't supposed to be back yet and why there was noise and guns and a party and a music-player and other things that belong to the Outside and why Father Prophet lives in the big house instead of a dorm and why his chairs are always bigger and covered in cushions while we crowd onto stone benches and why no one in the Girls' Dorm woke up even when I made all of that noise and why Father let Louis take me to begin with.

I'm seconds away from it all making sense.

"Judge me worthy," I say to Mother God, like I'm supposed to, like I've seen so many girls do before. And I know she will.

Then, slowly, I raise my arms, close my eyes, and wait for them to be accosted by electric lights.

Too many seconds go by before I realize I'm standing with my arms ahead of me and my eyes shut for nothing. It's dark. The sun is barely touching the windows anymore. It's empty and dark.

It didn't work.

It has to work. I know it will work.

"Judge me worthy," I say again, louder this time.

I close my eyes and my hands come up. I freeze like that. Turn them on! *Turn them on! Turn them on!* I beg her in my skull. Nothing.

Then the door behind me clicks open. Not the one at the

back of the Chapel that we all enter through. The one at the front. The one only Father Prophet ever uses. I don't open my eyes to look, but I know Father's here. He's changed his mind. He knows that I thought about him every day and I want nothing but to be full of Light.

Maybe that thing in his house was my final test.

I keep my eyes closed as I listen to his footsteps cross the stage and stop next to his chair. I expect to hear him sit, but when he doesn't, I do it again anyway.

"Judge me worthy!" I practically shout it. Then my hands go up and BOOM. I don't even need to open my eyes to know it. They're on fire. There are lights everywhere, shining from the floor, the ceiling, the walls, the stage, the benches. The entire room is full of buzzing, electric light.

I did it.

Relief floods every inch of my veins. My breath rushes cool out my nose. My smile slices my face in half.

I open my eyes and at first I can't see anything but a wall of light so bright it makes them ache.

I squint and turn, ready to see Father, ready to run straight into his arms and hug him.

But he's not there.

He's not in his chair or next to his chair or anywhere in the Chapel.

Instead, crouching there in Mother's Chapel, next to Father's chair, with a hand snaked between two of Father's pillows, is Louis.

Tears come to my eyes. My body deflates. My spine can't hold me up anymore. My lungs are burning. My legs are jelly.

"Zylynn," Louis says. He moves one of the pillows so that I can see something. "It's a light switch."

It's there, right in his fingers. Even though it can't be. It's there. It's a light switch.

I didn't turn the lights on. But no one has turned the lights on.

Ever.

Every Ceremony has been a lie.

My whole life every light has been nothing but electricity.

The lights are on but the world goes dark.

I collapse.

Twenty-Six

THE NEXT THING I FEEL IS the water as it slides through my mouth and slips into my stomach.

"We have to get her out of here."

A voice floats over my head. A man's voice. Not Louis's.

I blink. Which means my eyes are open. I didn't turn on the lights but I'm still alive. My eyes still open.

No one has ever turned on the lights. It's a light switch.

I'm sitting on the edge of the stage, my feet hanging off it. I'm leaning against Louis, which is OK because if I wasn't I would fall off onto the benches. He's keeping me safe. I blink at his eyes. He kept me safe. Louis, the Outsider, the Liar. I don't move from his arm.

"Zylynn? You OK, sweetheart?" the other voice says.

I turn. It's Uncle Alan. He's squatting next to me, holding a water bottle close to my mouth.

I'm not OK, I don't think. I didn't turn the lights on. There weren't any lights to turn on. Every ceremony I've ever been to has been nothing, pointless. My whole life has been pointless. Father Prophet yelled at me like that and it wasn't a test. He ate food and had a feast on a Hungry Day. He had a gun in his house.

Father Prophet was the only person I ever trusted. And he was a Liar.

I'm not OK.

But I'm here.

It's dark in the Chapel, but I can still breathe. My skin is not burning.

Mother God has kept me alive for one more day or year or something.

"Zy-baby," Louis says. He squeezes my shoulders and I smell his skin, then I remember: he's been here before. With me. He's held a tiny version of me here in this Chapel.

So once, a long time ago, he was someone else who I trusted. Once, a long time ago, I trusted him to hold me up through a whole Chapel service, and he did.

"I'd like to take you home now. Is that all right?" Louis says.

I know that he doesn't mean my home; he doesn't mean back to the Girls' Dorm to drink pomegranate tea and sleep until waking up for a scratchy-soap shower and breakfast and school. He means his home. In Darkness.

But even in Darkness there's electricity and light switches. There's also birthday cake and little sisters and Turtles. Maybe the Darkness isn't the Darkness after all.

I nod.

I'm so weak it takes both of the men, all of their muscles under my arms, to help me walk out of the Chapel. And once we're in the second circle, Louis says, "Hey, Zylynn, those legs must be tired. How about a piggyback ride?" I'm too exhausted to wonder what that is. I let him hoist me on his back and I only watch the world, my world, go by.

Good-bye, classrooms and Exercise Fields and offices and buildings I don't know what you're for. Good-bye, circles and clay paths and Dining Hall and Men's Dorm and Teen Girls' Dorm and Teen Boys' Dorm and Boys' Dorm and my dorm. Good-bye, Chapel. Good-bye, walls and hedges and dogs. Good-bye, home.

I know I'll never see it again.

"Zylynn," Uncle Alan whispers. "I'm so sorry we didn't find you sooner. I'm sorry you had such a hard day in the heat with no food."

"I had an orange and a chocolate bar and a tomato and some cheese," I whisper.

Uncle Alan nods. I see the corners of his mouth turn up then down then up then down. "We should have found you sooner. We should have looked here right away. I'm sorry we didn't protect you," Louis says. I feel his voice moving through his back as he carries me through the compound.

"We went to your friend Jaycia's house," Uncle Alan says. "When you weren't there, we asked her where you might be. She swore up and down that you'd never come back here. She said you'd talked last night."

I'm too tired to feel guilty about lying to Jaycia, but somewhere in me, I know I should. I know I'll feel guilty about it eventually.

"She had us searching Target and the mall and the park and the restaurant. We were so panicked. We couldn't find you anywhere. We didn't know what to do until Elsie told us you had tried to take her with you to your ceremony."

"We've been searching for you all day," Louis says. I can feel the vibrations of his voice through his back. "I'm so glad we found you."

"We found you just before you got to the compound gate."

I squint at Uncle Alan. The sun is gone now but there's spotlights shining from each building so I can see his yellow beard. Like my hair. Like Thesmerelda's.

"You didn't find me until I got to the Chapel," I say. I don't want the lying to start now.

He smiles. "Did you see a green van pass you just before you found the gate?"

> **Van** (n.): a boxlike vehicle that often has double doors both at the rear and along the sides; can be fitted with seats or used as a truck

"Yes," I say.

"That's my car," he says.

"We realized we had seen you too late, so we turned back and started searching. Then we finally saw you walking toward the walls. We were about to catch up to you but the dogs stopped us a bit at the gate. How do we get past them on the way out?"

I sigh against Louis's back. "They never stop you from going out. Only going in," I say.

It's another thing that doesn't make sense, I realize. Why should coming to the Light be scarier than leaving it? Why should entering Inside be more dangerous than going away from it?

Nothing in my life has made sense. How is that something I never noticed before?

Still, as we cross that gate, as the dogs lie there unmoving, I'm crying. It's my home. I'm going to miss it, even though I'm not sure if I should.

In the van, Uncle Alan sits in the driver's seat and Louis sits next to him. I'm on the bench behind them with my legs sprawled across it. My feet are red and swollen like I got stung by a wasp on my ankles and heels and big toes.

We're parked on a stretch of land a few yards from the compound entrance.

"Oh no!" I say. Uncle Alan and Louis both spin their heads around.

"What?" Louis asks.

"I forgot my shoes and socks!"

Louis laughs. "Don't worry about that," he says. "We'll buy you new sneakers."

He's lying. I can't help but think he's lying.

Then Uncle Alan unzips something. He says, "What did

you say you've had to eat all day? A tomato and some cheese?"

"And an orange and a chocolate bar," I say.

Louis chuckles but I can tell it's not a real laugh. It's the kind of laugh I made Inside: he put it there on purpose. "Here," he says. He reaches a hand back to me. In it is a turkey sandwich on brown bread with lettuce and tomato and mayonnaise peeking out the sides. "Eat. Your body is desperate for protein. Once you eat that, there are a bunch of strawberries in this cooler."

It's in my hands and then it's in my mouth and it's real. Not a lie.

"There will still be food?" I say.

Uncle Alan starts the car. Louis turns to look at me.

"Even now that I'm thirteen there will still be food in Darkness?"

Louis reaches a hand toward my knee but when I flinch he leaves it hanging there, a broken tree branch off the back of his seat. "Zylynn," he says. "I promise you. You will never have another Hungry Day again."

And I know, this time I know—maybe Mother God tells me or maybe there's a little piece of me that belongs only to me that somehow knows—he's telling the truth.

My eyes are spilling over. My home is disappearing out the back window. My stomach is getting fuller and fuller and it will never be empty again.

I don't know how to thank him. I don't know if I should thank him.

I reach out and brush a finger against that hanging hand. And he smiles.

"I'm supposed to protect you, you know," he says. "I'm your dad."

Louis takes his phone out of his pocket when we pull onto the street with Charita and Elsie and Junior and Jakey and Louis's house at the end of it. My house at the end of it.

"We'll be there in under a minute, babe," I hear him say.

He's talking to Charita.

I feel stronger now with bottle after bottle of water and a sandwich and strawberries in my belly. Strong enough to wonder. Curiosity perches softly on my shoulder. I let her stay.

How did Louis and Thesmerelda end up Inside in the first place? Why is Thesmerelda still there if there's food out here and the Darkness doesn't burn you like Father said it would? Why did Father . . . lie?

I watch the houses fly by the window so much faster than they did this morning. I won't sit still in the chair in the Pink Stripes Room anymore. I won't sit at my window anymore. I won't watch this street and force Father to come walking up it searching for me. He's not coming. I'm staying here. In Darkness.

Except it's only dark at night. Like now. And the dark isn't even hurting me.

Uncle Alan drives into the driveway.

Louis turns to look at me. "I'm so sorry, Zylynn. I never

should have left you there," he says. Then he takes a deep breath. "A long time ago, I used to live Inside too," he says.

"I know," I say.

"Oh!" Louis says. "You figured that out?"

I nod.

"Look, I should have taken you with me. Back when I first left, I should have kept you with me. My head was still all screwed up and I thought leaving you with your mother the best thing to do. Plus, it wasn't as bad back then, eight years ago. But . . . we had Hungry Days."

"Is that why you left?"

He sighs. "I'll tell you the whole story sometime. But now let's get inside."

"No," I say. There must have been more strength than I thought hiding in the layers of that turkey sandwich. "Now. Tell me now."

This is the story, the real story, of where I come from. And I need to hear it. To know it. To repeat it in my brain until it makes sense.

Uncle Alan turns to me now too. "Zylynn, we have—"

I cut him off. "Please tell me. Now. Please. I have to know now." I swallow hard. Then I add, "Dad."

Louis/Dad looks at Uncle Alan and he sighs and nods and gets out of his van and goes in the house. Louis/Dad gets out of the car like he did that first night and this time I know he's only coming to my door. He opens it. "Scoot over," he says.

He sits next to me on the bench in the middle of Uncle

Alan's van and I watch letters dance in his eyes and I breathe and I sip water and I wait because I know he'll tell me and I know he's not lying now.

"Your mother and I were young and in love and stupid," he starts.

I gasp. I thought I was the only one who worried about being stupid.

"This isn't going to be easy for you to understand, OK? Because you grew up really differently from anyone I know. So listen, get the bits of it you can, OK, sweetie? I will tell you this story as many times as I need to year after year until you understand it all."

I nod. Year after year. He's going to be with me year after year.

"I was young. Older than you, but not much. Nineteen. And I met your mother."

"Thesmerelda," I whisper.

Louis's green eyes go big. "You figured it out," he says slowly. "I mean they said you would but . . ."

We pause for a second before he goes on.

"We were instantly a pair, Tessie and me. That's what we called her before we went and joined the Children Inside. We both hated everything about the way we'd been raised. We hated the world. For no good reason, really. It's not like we were particularly damaged or anything. No. Your uncle doesn't understand this. Your stepmother either. But it could happen to anyone. Anyone."

I don't know what he's talking about but I think I get the part where I'm supposed to pick up what I can for now, so I nod.

"Jim had some things to say. Some things about greed and violence and how to fight it. Some things that made me listen. Tessie too."

"Jim?" I ask.

Louis/Dad laughs. "You call him Father Prophet. His Outside name—his real name—is Jim."

"Jim?" I'm smiling too for some reason. Not a little pinch-y smile, but a huge one that threatens to tear my cheeks in order to get big enough. A smile made of relief. He's not nearly so big and scary and powerful as I thought. His name is only Jim.

My name is more powerful than his.

"Anyway, we liked what he had to say about abandoning belongings and going after the truth."

"And the Light," I add.

Louis/Dad shakes his head. "The Light stuff came later. The Hungry Days came later. That horrible drugged tea came later too."

The smile dies on my face and rots. "The tea had drugs in it?" I ask. My eyes are wide.

Louis/Dad nods. "To make you sleep. It took so long for me to figure it out."

I chew my cheek. "I drank it every night," I whisper.

Louis/Dad deflates. "I'm so sorry, Zylynn. I'm so sorry."

I shake my head. "Keep going."

"By the time he started the really kooky stuff, I went along with it. We'd given him all of our money. We'd moved Inside. We lived together then, though. None of this keeping the men and women apart except for one week every few months. None of this using the women as Gatherers. None of these rules about how you can't choose to love one particular woman—or even your own particular child for God's sake—differently than all the rest of the people. All that started after I left. And there weren't as many lightbulbs and there weren't as many Hungry Days, I'm certain." He sighs. "Anyway, after we were there awhile, you were born."

"Where was Charita?" I ask.

Louis/Dad tilts his head at me. "I didn't know her yet, sweetie. I didn't know her until after I left."

"You've known me longer? Than Charita?"

Dad/Louis takes my chin in his palm. His touch is so much softer than Father's. Than Jim's. "Zylynn, baby, I've known you and I've loved you since the second you were born. When I lived on the compound, we lived like a family. You and your mother and me. Mom and Dad and baby. We loved each other. We took care of each other. We talked and hugged and laughed every day. That's what families—moms and dads and daughters and sons and brothers and sisters—are supposed to do."

"Like you and Charita and Junior and Elsie and Jakey," I say. "You're a family."

"And you," Dad/Louis says, blinking a lot to keep the tears

from getting past his eyelashes. "And you. You're also our daughter and sister. You were always missing and now you're not."

We freeze like that for a second. It's not until Dad/Louis's hand gets wet that I realize I'm crying too.

"Anyway," he says. "I knew I had to get out of there. But your mother still loved it so much. She was so happy with giving everything up to be a part of the Movement. I was being suffocated by it while she was lit on fire. I didn't want to take that from her."

He gulps.

"And she . . . she was more important to you than I was. Back then. She was . . . so good. With you, I mean. You were on her hip all day and all night. You were laughing and singing and . . . God, what happened?"

Now he's crying way past his eyelashes.

I think about her. Thesmerelda.

"She sits in the corner," I say.

Louis stops crying to squint at me. "What?"

"Thesmerelda. Now. She sits in a corner." I pause before I try the words on my tongue. "My mother."

Louis leans toward me. "How do you know that?"

"I saw her tonight. At Fath—Jim's house," I say.

Dad/Louis's eyes are so big I'm sure they're going to pop out of his head and splat right into my forehead. "You went to his house? Tonight?"

I nod. "He always said so much about drugs. Father. Jim.

Drugs are everywhere on the Outside causing darkness. And guns. And violence. And greed."

"I know," Louis says.

"But I saw some of those things tonight. In Father Prophet's living room."

"Oh, Zylynn," Dad/Louis says. "I'm so sorry. It's going to take a long time for you to fully heal, but you're safe now, I promise."

"Will she always sit in that corner?" I ask.

He sighs. "I don't know," he says. "I hope that eventually people will see the truth behind Jim and the compound and shut it down. Or that maybe your mother will take enough nights off from the tea to figure it out and leave. I hope so. But I don't know when that will happen. I don't know if it will."

I nod.

"What did she say? What did he say?" Dad/Louis asks.

"She—" Except I can't say anything. I can't admit that she let me go. I can't explain that her words, weak and stringy and quiet, were enough. I can't promise I saw her eyes happy I was escaping because I only really saw them with my imagination, but I knew they were there. So instead I tell Dad/Louis about what Jim said. It's not as awful to remember when I get to call him Jim.

At the end Dad/Louis says, "He was lying, Zylynn. He was always lying. I can't believe I let him take over all of our lives."

"What?"

He sighs. "This is so hard to explain and it's late but I'll try. I won, OK? About a year ago, the Inside doctor—you called him Brother Tomlinkin—he ran away from the compound and spread the truth about what was happening there to every news outlet he could find. He's a hero, that man. It woke me up. I went to court. It killed me to do it, but I sued your mother for full custody of you. And I won. That means that until you're an adult—eighteen, not thirteen—I'm in charge of you. I have to keep you fed and safe and protected and, yes, loved. That's the job of a mother and a father and I'm so sorry your mother isn't up to it, OK? But you've got a father here. A dad, not a prophet. And I'm going to do my best."

There are so many tears falling from the four eyes in the car I'm sure we'll drown in them before we go in the house.

"So he couldn't let you stay," Dad/Louis says. "Jim was forbidden from letting you stay. He made you believe you'd messed up only because the courts, the government, they have more power than one silly little guy who calls himself a prophet and they said you can't go back there. They said it would be best for you to stay here with me and Charita."

There are so many things here. Some I get. Some make no sense. But Curiosity is off my shoulder. She's lying at my feet, ready to wake up when I have more energy. Ready to feed me questions all day or week or year until Dad/Louis and Charita have answered them all.

For now, I only have one more question. "Does Thesmerelda have to be my only mother?"

Dad/Louis squints. "You can still think of God as your Mother if you want."

My head is shaking. Tears are flying off my face right and left and left and right. "No, no, no," I say. "I mean . . . can Charita be my mother too?"

Louis reaches for me and this time I let him hug me. This time his arms feel safe. "Let's go ask her, OK?" he says.

Dad/Louis keeps his hand on my shoulder we walk up the sidewalk toward the front door of their house. My house. Our house.

I'm OK with his palm on me; I'm OK with him leading me forward. I'm OK.

I'm not sure if I trust him because I trust him or only because I don't have any other choice. I'm not sure if I should trust him. I'm not sure if Mother God would want me to trust him. I'm not sure if Mother God is real anymore.

The tears are almost back by the time we climb the front steps.

"Hey?" he says. He tugs on my arm until I'm facing him. "This is a lot of serious stuff, huh?" he says.

I nod.

"And you and me, kid, we need each other. We're the people who learned the truth. We're the people who made it out of there."

He winks.

I smile.

"We'll figure it out together, OK?"

I nod.

"But sometimes we need to forget the serious stuff and just have a little bit of fun, OK?"

Fun. I look at my bare feet. My brain spins until it lands on a picture of Jaycia. She's so clear in my imagination. Laughing in her bed after telling that skeleton joke. Throwing her head back so her translucent blond hair reached toward her pillow. Fun.

She made it out too. She can be my friend in Darkness. Or whatever this is.

Except I have to call her Janice now. She's Janice.

"And Zylynn?" Louis says.

I look up at his eyes again. Just like mine. "Yeah?" I say.

He smiles, a big one. "Happy birthday."

I'm smiling too as we step into the dark house, just like we did ten days ago. Except as soon as my foot hits the floor, the lights go on, like I stepped on a light switch.

"SURPRISE!" Three little voices shout it.

I look up to see Elsie and Jakey and Junior and Uncle Alan and Charita all sitting around the coffee table with the HAPPY BIRTHDAY ZYLYNN banner hanging over their heads and a pink cake glowing with candles lighting up the underside of all of their faces.

I'm smiling.

They're singing.

"Happy birthday, dear Zylynn, happy birthday to you."

By the time they stop singing, Elsie is wound around my leg. "You came back!" she squeals. "You came back!"

I want to tell her of course I did. I was always going to come back. But I know when I left this morning, I was planning to come back so that I could take her with me. I want to think I never would have done that, but I would have. I want to think I would never throw a rock at a kid because he ate extra oatmeal. I want to think I never would drink a cup of tea with drugs in it. But I did. Maybe Louis rescued me from my own brain.

I will never have to do those things again.

I do something I've never done before. I lift Elsie up and plop her on my hip, just like Charita does.

"We missed you," Junior says.

"Mommy and Daddy let us get up in the middle of the night just to sing to you and eat cake!" Elsie's fingers are in my hair now. "Because it's your birthday, right, sis?"

My smile is so big my cheeks ache and I almost can't get the words out.

"I'm thirteen," I say.

Junior comes up and puts a hand on my shoulder. "Where were you today?"

Then Charita is there, with Jakey on her hip and her arms around all of us. Louis puts his arms around her and then he is on the outside of the hug and everybody in the house is squishing together in his arms and it feels so good I think my smile might break my face in half.

Click. Click. Click. Uncle Alan and the camera circle us: more pages for my book.

"But where were you?" Junior says again, his words smushed in the middle of the biggest hug ever.

"It doesn't matter where she went, sweetie. She's right where she should be," Charita says.

The hug gets extra tight, and then it's gone. Only Elsie still on my hip.

We all freeze like that, staring and smiling, until Jakey shouts, "Give me cake!"

The laugh that comes out of me is so different this time. Big and round and happy.

It's a real laugh.

And it's mine.

Acknowledgments

Thank you will never be enough, but it's a start. So here we go.

Thank you to my incredible agent, Kate McKean, for believing in my books, for believing in Zylynn, and for not calling me crazy when I said I was writing a children's book about cults.

Karen Chaplin, my brilliant editor, thank you for "getting" Zylynn and her story from the start, for embracing the dark parts of my brain, for making every page of this book better. And for making me a better writer, too!

Thank you to everyone else at Harper. I have felt your support through every step of this process. Special thanks to Olivia Russo, to everyone in sales and marketing, and of course to Erin Fitzsimmons for the absolutely perfect cover!

My early readers, your encouragement was priceless when Zylynn and I were just getting to know each other. Thank you, Alison Cherry, Alyson Gerber, Dhonielle Clayton, Amy Ewing, Corey Ann Haydu, and Allary Montague. Thank you to The New School, the Lucky 13s, The Class of 2k13, and all my fabulous writer friends and teachers.

To cult survivors: thank you. If you shared your story,

believe me, I found it. I am awed by your bravery and resilience. Thank you for sharing your words or videos or interviews. I hope Zylynn's story honors yours.

Thank you to my family: Beth Carter for your deep life insights, your enthusiastic reading, and for being a wonderful mom; Bill Carter for your unwavering support, for the intellectual conversations that I think started the moment I was born, and for being a funny dad and a great dad, too; Dan Carter for being the best brother a writer could ask for. Thank you to my in-laws, aunts, uncles, and cousins. I have so much family support I can practically swim in it.

To my students, past and present: thank you for your unique view of the world, for your trust, and your brilliance. I love you all.

A special thank you to these wonderful people in my life whose support I can always count on in so many ways: Dahlia Adler, Katherine Aragon and Seth Berkowitz, Paul Bausch, Kate Beck, Megan Burke and Joe Mrak, Alexandra Carter and Greg Lembrich, John Carter, Rich and Brittany Carter, Molly and Mike Colonna, Malick Fall, Gia Jimenez, Melissa Heinold, Linda Hu and Nestor Alvarado, Andy Kabala, Chemagne and Greg Kania, Sarah and Bill Kirk, Ronnie and Eric Larsson, Eileen Larsson, Eric and Lauren Larsson, Tom Larsson, Erin Larsson, Kristin and Zach LeFeber, Caron Levis, David Levithan, Mary Lou and Diego Merida, Jenn and Jason Meyers, Catherine and Dan O'Neill, Bridget O'Neill, Danny O'Neill, Riddhi Parekh, Caitlin and Jeff Platzman, Mindy

Raf, Lindsay Ribar, Anna and Tim Rosenwong, Frank Scallon, Betsy Schroeder and Erin Yanovich, Mary G. Thompson, and Aaron and Stacy Wall.

It's a special thing when your writer-friends become your regular-life-friends too. Amy Ewing, Corey Haydu, Alyson Gerber, and Jess Verdi: thank you for your insights in writing and in life. I'm lucky to have you.

And of course, biggest thanks to my strongest supporter, my closest confidant, my partner and my love: Greg Larsson, you're simply the best.